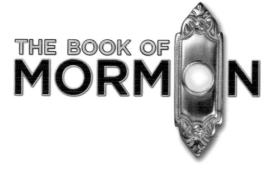

"★★★★★ A heavenly musical. Oh boy, it's a real winner. The show is blissfully original, irreverent, outspoken and hilarious. And all that's tucked inside a good — no, great — old-fashioned musical. It's a show where you catch yourself laughing one minute, mouth agape the next, eventually wiping away tears and, finally, cheering. Polished and exuberant and surging with surprises, and amazingly fun with enormous wit and imagination. This musical spills over with confidence in the material and cast. There is such infectious energy you want to join in onstage. Being among the converted is what it's all about. A fantastic musical in every way. Sheer joy."

NEW YORK DAILY NEWS JOE DZIEMIANOWICZ

"*The Book of Mormon* manages to offend, provoke laughter, trigger eye-rolling, satirize convention and warm hearts, all at the same time. An inventive, subversive, rollicking show. You might expect Parker, Stone and Lopez to utterly disrespect traditional musical conventions, but you'd be wrong. What they've done is carefully maintain the structure and rhythm of a classic musical – think Rodgers and Hammerstein's *The King and I* – even while filling it with utter zaniness. Ultimately, believe it or not, this is a pro-religion musical, or at least a story about the uplifting power of stories. Far from being nihilistic, the moral seems to endorse any belief system – no matter how crazy it sounds – if it helps us do good. Amen to that. Consider us converted."

AP MARK KENNEDY

"Anyone who saw *South Park: Bigger, Longer & Uncut* shouldn't be surprised to learn that Trey Parker and Matt Stone appear genuinely to love musicals even as they subvert them. What's perhaps less expected is that while *The Book of Mormon* packs plenty of blissful profanity, sacrilege and politically incorrect mischief, the defining quality of this hugely entertaining show is its sweetness. One of the freshest original musicals in recent memory. It has tuneful songs, clever lyrics, winning characters, explosive laughs and disarmingly intimate moments. The show manages to have a comic field day with Mormonism while simultaneously acknowledging – maybe even respecting – the right of everyone to follow any faith they choose. Or invent. Number after number hits a bull's-eye. In terms of construction and song placement, *Mormon* masters a classic formula. What makes the musical irresistible, however, is its panache in making naughty mockery of a whole string of untouchable subjects, without an ounce of spite."

HOLLYWOOD REPORTER DAVID ROONEY

"Behold *The Book of Mormon*. An exhilarating Broadway musical at once revolutionary and classic, hilarious and humane, funny and obscene, uncompromising in production standards and unafraid of just about anything. A spectacular, rather perfect Broadway musical not only grounded in a serious love and understanding of the traditions that make a Broadway musical great but also filled with love for the very flawed, mortal characters who populate this romp. This is what 21st-century Broadway can be. If Broadway has the balls. Lord knows, *The Book of Mormon* does. I'm sold; I believe in *The Book of Mormon*."

ENTERTAINMENT WEEKLY LISA SCHWARZBAUM

"If any show could make the case that you can have fun with absolutely anything in the oft-painful run of human experience, then that show is *The Book of Mormon*, a shrewd, remarkably well-crafted and wholly hilarious new Broadway musical. By the end of a night more emotional than many will expect, the show is arguing the importance of finding a spiritual center, if not exactly embracing the doctrinal details of that most American of religions. And *The Book of Mormon* even makes a case that it takes those suffering real pain to understand the real role of religion in our lives."

CHICAGO TRIBUNE CHRIS JONES

"A hilarious musical. *The Book of Mormon* is gleefully funny. It seldom goes more than 10 seconds without a big laugh. And it's not just about the jokes. They're embedded in a satisfying story, supported by witty, character-relevant songs. Most important for its overall success, the show's creators understand that even a satirical musical needs to have characters you can care about. *Mormon* is that rare creature that isn't based on a book or a play or a movie – it came totally out of its creators' heads. And what they thought up is one of the most purely enjoyable musicals in years."

BERGEN RECORD ROBERT FELDBERG

"Do you believe in theater, friend? Or has your faith been strained to the breaking point? If so, I say unto thee, go forth to the tabernacle otherwise known as the Eugene O'Neill Theatre! It's an often uproarious, spiritually up-tempo satire not just of Mormonism, and not just religion in general, but of (no kidding) Occidental civilization itself, in all its well-intentioned, self-mythologizing, autoerotically entitled glory. *Mormon* chipperly shitcans all pieties... Except the sacred, mystic conventions of musical theater. What's so uniquely winning about *The Book of Mormon* is its scruffy humanism, its eagerness to redeem its characters – even its smaller ones. When Lieutenant Uhura, Frodo, Yoda, Jesus, Satan, Joseph Smith, Darth Vader, and the Angel Moroni all converge to sanctify a show, that's what I call a quorum. After *Mormon*, I like to imagine, the Broadway musical might be free to be a Broadway musical again."

NEW YORK MAGAZINE SCOTT BROWN

"Boisterously outrageous. It's hard to imagine anyone topping the ding-dong hilarity set off by *The Book of Mormon*. It has all the fearlessness one would expect. Sacred cows, let's just say, are there for the riotous milking. But for all its irreverence, *The Book of Mormon* has the old-fashioned musical comedy heart of adults who spent much of their adolescence lip-syncing to original cast albums in their finished basements. Nothing is off limits. The farcical stampede is unstoppable. It's not easy to shock a modern-day audience, but *The Book of Mormon* succeeds with alarming regularity. *The Book of Mormon* has the propulsive verve of a runaway hit."

LOS ANGELES TIMES CHARLES MCNULTY

"★★★★★ Musical-comedy heaven. If theater is your religion and the Broadway musical your sect, you've been woefully faith-challenged of late. *The Book of Mormon* is a sick mystic revelation, the most exuberantly entertaining Broadway musical in years. In fact, the uses and abuses of faith, the strange persistence of these ancient (or in the case of Mormonism, not so ancient) bedtime stories, is a central theme. Religion, the creators firmly point out, is showbiz, and the satire bites into both the absurdities of Joseph Smith and his angel Moroni, and the intoxicating frivolity of musicals. A show that examines, with impressive insight, cultural transmission, adaptation, and assimilation. It's about our ineradicable hunger for narrative and mystery. A viciously hilarious treat."

TIME OUT NEW YORK DAVID COTE

"Matt and Trey: Where have you been all my life? Along with Robert Lopez, Stone and Parker have devised *The Book of Mormon*, a pricelessly entertaining act of musical comedy subversion. The mighty O'Neill himself would have to have given it up for this extraordinarily well-crafted musical assault on all things holy. The marvel of *The Book of Mormon* is that even as it profanes some serious articles of faith, its spirit is anything but mean. One of the most joyously acidic bundles Broadway has unwrapped in years. The sin it takes such fond aim at – blind faith – is one that this musical suggests observes no religious bounds. No matter how brazenly the writers question the precepts of Mormonism – and boy, do they ever make mincemeat of the religion's genesis – their respect for the traditions of the American musical borders on devotional."

WASHINGTON POST PETER MARKS

"★★★★ A fiendishly well-crafted, hilariously smart – or maybe smartly hilarious – song-and-dance extravaganza. The show's a hoot. The show's a hit. A full-blooded tuner that rejuvenates musicals while displaying a genuine love for the form. An avalanche of filthy gags, butt jokes and wickedly catchy show tunes. Each time you think they can't possibly top a particularly crazed moment, 10 more follow. By the time *The Book of Mormon* ends in an orgy of over-the-top cheer, you just can't wait to get on that ride all over again."

NEW YORK POST ELIZABETH VINCENTELLI

"This is to all the doubters and deniers out there, the ones who say that heaven on Broadway does not exist, that it's only some myth our ancestors dreamed up. I am here to report that a newborn, old-fashioned, pleasure-giving musical has arrived at the Eugene O'Neill Theatre, the kind our grandparents told us left them walking on air if not on water. So hie thee hence, nonbelievers (and believers too), to *The Book of Mormon*, and feast upon its sweetness. *The Book of Mormon* achieves something like a miracle. Trust me when I tell you that its heart is as pure as that of a Rodgers and Hammerstein show. These men take pleasure in the transcendent, cathartic goofiness of song-and-dance numbers. Witty, ridiculous, impeccably executed, genuinely stirring. All the folks involved in *Mormon* prove themselves worthy, dues-paying members of the church of Broadway. A celebration of the privilege, for just a couple of hours, of living inside that improbable paradise called a musical comedy."

NEW YORK TIMES BEN BRANTLEY

"Wildly original, jubilant and expert. Everything you should expect from a show by the heat-seeking rascals of *South Park*. What you may not expect, however, is the sweetness. An outcasts' love letter to musical theater. And for all the ridicule bludgeoned on the faithful, the musical seems smitten with the basic desire – however twisted and self-deluded – to do good."

NEWSDAY LINDA WINER

"A raucously funny new show. Every song enhances the hilarity, expert staging heightens every gag, and the cast of fresh faces is blissfully good. A show that never quits. For all its sacrilegious jabs, the show is earnestly about the power of faith. The Ugandan natives believe, and ultimately embrace religion, while the heroes realize that doctrine is all metaphor – 'a bunch of made-up stuff, but it points to something bigger.' And that describes *The Book of Mormon*, an original made-up-for-Broadway production that approaches musical-comedy Rapture."

VARIETY STEVEN SUSKIN

"The most surprising thing about *Mormon* may be its inherent sweetness. There is an exuberance in the show's spirit that makes it feel both fresh and unabashedly traditional. Makes us laugh and cheer."

USA TODAY ELYSA GARDNER

"★★★★ History is made. They had me at 'Hello'. It should keep audiences in shock and awe for years. The funniest show on Broadway by far, it's on its march into legend. But Parker and Stone also show an un-ironic compassion for the fallible humans caught in the web of religious hypocrisy. *The Book of Mormon* is as good as it gets. Come on *Mormons*, go into your dance."

ROLLING STONE PETER TRAVERS

"Parker and Stone's *The Book of Mormon* may offend thousands, if not more. And bless their iconoclastic hearts for it! It grabs the audience by the lapels and won't let go. Parker and Stone are actually morality-minded believers. The pair, who would seem to have made a career of contending that nothing's sacred, eventually suggest that something definitely is. They send a message that while organized religion — based on trumped up dogma, as it too often is — may be a stultifying and questionable experience for many, there is decidedly something behind truly religious behavior. It's based, they suggest, on conciliatory aspects that draw people together rather than force them apart."

HUFFINGTON POST DAVID FINKLE

"Rarely has a show come along as consummately crafted as *The Book of Mormon*. Adhering to all the Broadway conventions, creators Trey Parker and Matt Stone, along with Robert Lopez, deliver a work that is brilliantly original, hysterically funny and tunefully irresistible. The plot, which is dense with twists and turns, unfolds with great clarity and is splendidly paced. The extended songs are not only melodic, they cleverly advance the narrative which by show's end completes a perfect and highly satisfying arc. All the while, the show achieves the near impossible. While it ingeniously spoofs the hypocrisy within the Mormon scriptures, it manages to leave you with a renewed sense of spiritual faith. *The Book of Mormon* is an inspired collaboration made in theater heaven."

NY1 ROMA TORRE

"A screamingly funny yet sharply insightful full-length take on religion. There are also pointed but loving tributes to musical comedy conventions, shockingly vulgar humor, and that rarity on Broadway these days: topical and effective satire. The authors are focusing their blisteringly boisterous lens on cultural stereotypes and the extremes of fundamentalist faith to demonstrate their absurdity. Ultimately, they acknowledge that the altruistic element within the Church of Jesus Christ of Latter-Day Saints and other religions is worth preserving. That they manage to do this without compromising their gleefully vicious vision is nothing short of miraculous."

BACKSTAGE DAVID SHEWARD

"It's something just spectacular. New, exciting, chance-taking, funny, inappropriate, filthy, beautifully staged, a great brilliant romp of a musical. It's hysterical. It's hysterical. It's hard to believe that a play this funny and this outrageous can have a kind of tenderness about it. One of the funniest, most original things I've seen on Broadway. This is fresh, it's original, it's invigorating. We're laughing at ourselves and the ridiculousness of so many things that we are taught to believe in. I couldn't even go to sleep last night 'cause I kept thinking of this stuff. This is a winner."

WOR JOAN HAMBURG

"The shocking thing about *The Book of Mormon* is that after all the production numbers that make searing fun of Mormonism, African culture, AIDS, terror, mainline religion and every Western creation myth – after all of that, the show ends up an unbridled celebration of faith. *The Book of Mormon* is a triumph – that's not too strong a word: For all its outrageous mockery, the show encourages you to appreciate whatever creation story gives you comfort and allows you to appropriate mystery."

PHILADELPHIA INQUIRER HOWARD SHAPIRO

"There is a dirty secret hidden within *The Book of Mormon.* Indeed, the infamously irreverent Trey Parker and Matt Stone offer foul language, obscene jokes and plenty to offend, especially should you be a Latter-Day Saint. But their fantastic show isn't just fun, funny and immensely enjoyable; it's also surprisingly — and here's the dirty word — wholesome. An old-fashioned, toe-tapping, optimistic Big Broadway Musical, a buddy story about a mismatched pair of young Mormon missionaries sent to Uganda to convert the benighted natives. It argues for the social value of religion — no matter how implausible and arguably invented the stories upon which a religion is based — while teaching (if winkingly) the old showbiz lesson that the golden boy can be flawed, and the young misfit, if only he believes in himself, can come back a star. The whole enterprise is also a comfortably traditional show, in the best sense. Messrs. Parker, Lopez and Stone's tuneful score is memorable and hummable, show music that tells stories, deepens characters and gets laughs. So this is the lesson of *The Book of Mormon*: the elusive trick to succeeding on Broadway today is to write a smart, funny, sweet show, insert tuneful songs and a talented cast and give it a great staging. Subversive, ain't it?"

NEW YORK OBSERVER JESSE OXFELD

BOOK, MUSIC AND LYRICS BY

Trey Parker, Robert Lopez & Matt Stone

Newmarket Press New York

Published by Newmarket Press
18 East 48th Street, New York, New York 10017
Tel: (212) 832-3575; Fax: (212) 832-3629; email: info@newmarketpress.com
www.newmarketpress.com

FIRST EDITION
10 9 8 7 6 5 4 3 2 1

ISBN: 978-1-55704-993-3 (paperback)

Library of Congress Catalog-in-Publication Data available upon request.

The authors of
THE BOOK OF MORMON wish to express their
profound gratitude to all of their tremendous and
gifted collaborators, both onstage and off.
Thank you.

CONTENTS

FOREWORD

by Mark Harris

About five minutes into the *The Book of Mormon*, the jaw of the woman sitting to my left dropped, her arched eyebrows took up residence about one inch higher than their usual position, and her face remained thus frozen for the rest of the show, an ossified mask of utter shock, what an Easter Island statue might look like if another Easter Island statue suddenly farted. Conversely, the woman sitting to my right was so convulsed with laughter that she had to cover her mouth so she wouldn't miss the next line. And the man in front of me was wiping away a tear during the final song, perhaps because he was unexpectedly moved, or maybe out of sheer adrenalized elation that yes, they had really pulled it off—a great pastiche of classic musical comedies that, by sheer force of talent, brains, commitment and originality, had become a great musical comedy itself. It is one of the many triumphs of *The Book of Mormon* that these various reactions are equally appropriate, and the fact that if you're lucky, you can experience all three of them—shock, delight and joy—at the same time is a testament to the spectacular feat that Trey Parker, Matt Stone and Robert Lopez have pulled off.

And what better way to kill all that fun than by taking away the music, the great performances, the dazzling design and choreography and just looking at the script? Ordinarily, I'd warn people away from spoiling their own fun this way, but reading *The Book of Mormon* turns out to be a wholly entertaining and edifying experience on its own—a mellower moment in which to appreciate that the exuberant, anarchic spirit of what the *South Park* guys and the gentleman from *Avenue Q* have created was not accomplished casually. The subtlety and suppleness of the architecture of this piece is the product of exacting, even painstaking work. It's almost impossible to make it look this easy, but that's what musical theater has to do. And there's no condescension to the form in this amazing work—rather, there's a reverent understanding that the genre is rich and roomy enough to accommodate acid social commentary and high-energy dance breaks, Jesus, Hitler, and Starbucks, classic heartfelt moments and things that I'd be tempted to call unsayable except that they say them. All of them. Often in rhymed couplets.

Some people—not many—have contended that what you're about to read is deeply unfair to Mormons (it's not nice to make fun of somebody's religion). A few others have suggested that the show is deeply unfair to Africa (it's not nice to make fun of somebody's continent). And these two arguments are another very good reason to read the script. While you do, it might be helpful to keep in mind G.K. Chesterton's famous maxim that "wit is a sword; it is meant to make people feel the point as well as see it." But you don't need a copy of Bartlett's Familiar Quotations (or, okay, Google) to understand, from these pages, that Parker, Stone and Lopez are certainly not interested in taking a flamethrower to the Church of Jesus Christ of Latter-Day Saints, or in evincing any contempt for or indifference to the plight of Africans. As is always true of the best satirists, they are merciless but never mean.

Ultimately, they're determined to go for the jugular only when it comes to one particular target. That target is us. What the creators of *The Book of Mormon* understand so brilliantly is an essential and underexplored contradiction in the American character: they revel in the conundrum that we love learning about mystical faraway places— whether Uganda, Orlando or Sal Tlay Ka Siti—but at the same time, we're so creeped out by anything or anyone that isn't just like us that we have to make up fairy tales about them (and sometimes about ourselves) to make everything feel okay again. But the simple primitive people are not so simple—and neither, it turns out, are the simple primitive missionaries. In song after song and scene after scene, this show knows how to find that exquisitely uncomfortable sweet spot, the precise place where sunny optimism shades into privileged smugness, where blind faith becomes oblivious cultism, where charity crosses the line into sanctimony. I'd be more than happy to explain how, in songs like "I Believe" and "I Am Africa" and "You and Me (But Mostly Me)," they pull it off. But first of all, I have no idea, and second, in this case, explanations are completely superfluous. The point is, they do it, and do it impeccably. You come out of *The Book of Mormon* so happy that you don't even resent the fact that a couple of times, you yourself got punched in the nose. That's not just great theater. That's great writing.

April 3, 2011

Mark Harris is a journalist and the author of PICTURES AT A REVOLUTION: FIVE MOVIES AND THE BIRTH OF THE NEW HOLLYWOOD.

AUTHORS' INTRODUCTION

TREY PARKER:

I remember one night in two-thousand-something, Matt and I went to see *Avenue Q*, and — we really had no idea what it was. We just heard it was this puppet thing. We were doing *Team America* at the time, and in our own puppet hell. So we were sitting there, and halfway through the first act, I was like, *Wow, this is actually really good, and Matt doesn't wanna leave*. That's amazing, you know? So we started really looking through the Playbill, and in the Playbill we saw a special thank you to us. It was very bizarre, because we thought, *Wait a minute. We don't even know these guys at all*. And so we watched the second act just going, *We love this*. And by the time the second act was over, I was thinking, *This is exactly the thing I've always dreamed about doing*. This is exactly the thing I've always aspired to do on Broadway, since I was a kid trying to write funny songs and acting in Rodgers & Hammerstein musicals in school and dreaming about Broadway. I was so excited by it. And then it happened purely by coincidence that Bobby showed up that night, and he came down and introduced himself.

And we were like, *That was amazing.* And we asked him, *Why are we in the special thanks?* He told us that when he saw the *South Park* movie, he said, *Wow, this is exactly the kinda thing I wanna do.* So it was — it was crazy, 'cause it was, like, Bobby being so influenced by us, and then us being so influenced — back by him. It was so exciting. And we went out that night, and obviously just hit it off so well that we started talking — and seeing that he shared a love for Mormons. It just became ridiculously obvious that we should team up and do something. Something about Mormons.

MATT STONE:

It really is one of those stories that doesn't sound true. It sounds like we're making it up just to get past this question. But it really did happen in a moment, when we met Bobby — Bobby Lopez — the night that Trey and I saw *Avenue Q.* We were in town, meeting about *Team America,* our puppet movie, in 2003 or 4. And Scott Rudin told us, *You know, there's this puppet musical on Broadway, and it's good.* So we went and saw it that night, and both of us — me and Trey — we just loved it. And we saw our names in the Playbill. Because I think Bobby had seen the *South Park* movie and took it as a big inspiration. So we're like, *Well, that's weird.*

And so somebody hooked us up that night and we went out for a drink. Bobby is about five years younger than Trey and me, so he was looking to us as, like, elder statesmen or something — totally unwarranted — like, *Hey, okay, you guys have been in the business a long time. What should I try to do next?* And so our pat, dopey answer to this is, *Well, what do you wanna do?* And he said, *I wanna do something about Joseph Smith and Mormons.* And we were like, *What? Wait a second. Nobody likes that stuff except for us, you know? Nobody.* Only me and Trey have ever talked about that.

ROBERT LOPEZ:

Well, it first started, I guess, when the *South Park* movie came out, because a week after that, the idea came to me for *Avenue Q.* I think it just kinda got me off my ass and, you know — I'd always wanted to do a musical where you laugh from beginning to end, where it's not just a — you know, I always think of a musical as — it's a concert. It's a play. And sometimes it's a dance show. And all those things have to be building, and serve a story. But I always wanted to do a show — where the laughs built in the same way as the music, the story, the dancing, the costumes, and all that stuff.

And the *South Park* guys got there first. I saw that movie — I remember it was the summer of '99 — and I just thought, *Oh my God, this is exactly what I want to be doing.* So I set out to do just that. And cut to four years later. *Avenue Q* was open on Broadway, just barely — we had barely opened. And I came in one night, and there were Matt and Trey sitting in the audience. Their movie was so inspirational to me. And all of their work — all their comedy and all their songs had pointed the way for me in my work, that — we had actually thanked them in our bio.

And they had seen that. So when I approached them, they were like, *Hey, what's going on?* I took them across the street to the bar. I remember we just hung out and hung out and hung out. And it was sort of an epic evening. The upshot of it was, they said, *What are you working on next?* And I said, *I'd like to do something about Joseph Smith.* I wanted to do a show about religion that sort of got a huge amount of laughs on how ridiculous the stories were, you know, religious stories and miracles. But I also hoped the story could contain a lot of emotion — if not a love story, then a religious one. After all, what is a church service but live stories and music in front of an audience? The best Broadway musicals achieve that same thrilling uplift.

So when I said *Joseph Smith*, they were like, *We've wanted to do that, too.* They had done a musical called *Alfred Packer* for their college project, I guess. And they thought they might follow it up with a Joseph Smith musical, but they just never did. But they had it in their heads to do some kind of Joseph Smith musical. And basically I said, *You know, if you guys wanna do that, that's fine. Because I'd really love to see what you do, more than what I would do.* And I meant it.

And they said, *No.*

Let's do it together.

March 27, 2011

PRODUCTION HISTORY

The Book of Mormon opened on Broadway on March 24, 2011 at the
Eugene O'Neill Theatre where it was presented by Anne Garefino, Scott
Rudin, Roger Berlind, Scott M. Delman, Jean Doumanian, Roy Furman,
Important Musicals LLC, Stephanie P. McClelland, Kevin Morris, Jon B.
Platt, Sonia Friedman Productions, and Stuart Thompson. It was directed
by Casey Nicholaw and Trey Parker with choreography by Casey Nicholaw.
The set design was by Scott Pask, the costume design was by Ann Roth, the
lighting design was by Brian MacDevitt, the sound design was by Brian
Ronan; the musical direction and vocal arrangements were by Stephen
Oremus, the orchestrations were by Larry Hochman and Stephen Oremus,
the dance music arrangements were by Glen Kelly; the music coordinator
was Michael Keller, the production stage manager was Karen Moore. The
cast was (in order of appearance):

Mormon	*Jason Michael Snow*
Moroni	*Rory O'Malley*
Elder Price	*Andrew Rannells*
Elder Cunningham	*Josh Gad*
Price's Dad	*Lewis Cleale*
Cunningham's Dad	*Kevin Duda*
Mrs. Brown	*Rema Webb*
Guards	*John Eric Parker, Tommar Wilson*
Mafala Hatimbi	*Michael Potts*
Nabulungi	*Nikki M. James*
Elder McKinley	*Rory O'Malley*
General	*Brian Tyree Henry*
Doctor	*Michael James Scott*
Mission President	*Lewis Cleale*
Ensemble	*Scott Barnhardt, Justin Bohon, Darlesia Cearcy, Kevin Duda, Asmeret Ghebremichael, Brian Tyree Henry, Clark Johnsen, John Eric Parker, Benjamin Schrader, Michael James Scott, Brian Sears, Jason Michael Snow, Lawrence Stallings, Rema Webb, Maia Nkenge Wilson, Tommar Wilson*

THE BOOK OF MORMON
ACT ONE

THE BOOK OF MORMON
ACT TWO

ENTR'ACTE
Orchestra

PROLOGUE: THE HILL CUMORAH

THE VILLAGE

"MAKING THINGS UP AGAIN"
Elder Cunningham & Company

THE DREAM

"SPOOKY MORMON HELL DREAM"
Elder Price & Company

THE VILLAGE / THE GENERAL'S CAMP

"I BELIEVE"
Elder Price

THE VILLAGE

"BAPTIZE ME"
Elder Cunningham & Nabulungi

DIRTY RIVER NEAR THE VILLAGE

"I AM AFRICA"
Elder McKinley, Missionaries & Ugandans

A KAFE IN KITGULI

OUTSIDE THE MORMON MISSIONARIES' LIVING QUARTERS

"JOSEPH SMITH AMERICAN MOSES"
Nabulungi & Ugandans

THE VILLAGE

"TOMORROW IS A LATTER DAY"
*Elder Price, Elder Cunningham,
Nabulungi & Company*

"HELLO"
(reprise)
Company

"FINALE"
Company

ACT 1

THE BOOK OF MORMON

- PROLOGUE -
THE HILL CUMORAH

The Mormon theme blares out of trumpets. Upstage there is a large picture frame, depicting a biblical scene from the Book of Mormon.

NARRATOR
Long ago, in the year of our Lord 326 AD, a great prophet is leader of the Nephite people in ancient Upstate New York. His name...is Mormon.

MORMON
I am Mormon. My people sailed here from Israel to create a new civilization. These golden plates tell of our people and how we met... with Jesus Christ.

Christ appears to Mormon.

JESUS
I am Jesus. Take care of your golden plates, Mormon, for soon, your entire civilization will be gone and nobody will remember you.

Christ leaves and Mormon begins to write and then dig.

NARRATOR
Just before the Nephite people were wiped out, Mormon gave the plates to his son, Moroni.

MORONI
I am Moroni, the last of my kind. I shall BURY the golden plates, father, and perhaps one day, someone very special will find them...

NARRATOR
And lo, Moroni buried the golden plates high on a hill. Centuries later, the golden plates were found, giving birth to the fastest growing religion today! A church that even now sends missionaries out... All over the world...

- MISSIONARY
TRAINING CENTER -

ELDER KEVIN PRICE, a young, dashing Mormon missionary in a white shirt and black tie, walks up with a big smile on his face, holding the Book of Mormon. He pantomimes ringing a doorbell, and we hear DING DONG!

HELLO!

ELDER PRICE
HELLO,
MY NAME IS ELDER PRICE,
AND I WOULD LIKE TO SHARE
   WITH YOU
THE MOST AMAZING BOOK.

A different Mormon missionary now steps forward on another part of the stage and pretends to

ring a bell. (DING DONG)

ELDER GRANT

HELLO,
MY NAME IS ELDER GRANT,
IT'S A BOOK ABOUT AMERICA
A LONG LONG TIME AGO.

(DING DONG) Yet another kid at a different area of the stage.

ELDER PRICE

IT HAS SO MANY AWESOME PARTS –

(DING DONG) A new missionary rings, but no answer.

ELDER PRICE

YOU SIMPLY WON'T BELIEVE
HOW MUCH THIS BOOK
CAN CHANGE YOUR LIFE!

(DING DONG, DING DONG, DONG DONG) Same kid with no answer, tries more.

ELDER GREEN

HELLO,
MY NAME IS ELDER GREEN.

AND I WOULD LIKE TO SHARE WITH
YOU THIS BOOK OF JESUS CHRIST.

(DING DONG)

ELDER YOUNG

HELLO, MY NAME IS ELDER
YOUNG.

ELDER HARRIS

HELLO!

ELDER YOUNG

DID YOU KNOW THAT JESUS
LIVED HERE IN THE USA?

ELDER GRANT

YOU CAN READ ALL ABOUT IT NOW.

ELDER CROSS

HELLO!

ELDER GRANT

IN THIS NIFTY BOOK, IT'S FREE!
NO YOU DON'T HAVE TO PAY.

ELDER YOUNG

HELLO!

ELDER SMITH
HELLO,
MY NAME IS ELDER SMITH,
AND CAN I LEAVE THIS BOOK
WITH YOU
FOR YOU TO JUST PERUSE?

ELDER BROWN
HELLO!

ELDER GREEN
HELLO!

ELDER HARRIS
HELLO!

ELDER SMITH
I'LL JUST LEAVE IT HERE.
IT HAS A LOT OF INFORMATION
YOU CAN REALLY USE.

ELDER PRICE
HELLO!

ELDER HARRIS
HI!

ELDER PRICE
MY NAME IS–

ELDER GREEN
JESUS CHRIST!

ELDER GRANT
YOU HAVE A LOVELY HOME

ELDER CROSS
HELLO!

ELDER YOUNG
IT'S AN AMAZING BOOK

ELDER SMITH
BONJOUR!

ELDER WHITE
HOLA!

ELDER HARRIS
NI HAO!

ELDER WHITE
ME LLAMO ELDER WHITE.

ELDER GRANT
ARE THESE YOUR KIDS?

ELDER GREEN
THIS BOOK GIVES YOU THE SECRET
TO ETERNAL LIFE.

ELDER CROSS
SOUND GOOD?

ELDERS
ETERNAL LIFE!

ELDER GREEN
WITH JESUS CHRIST!

ELDERS
IS SUPER FUN!

ELDER WHITE
HELLO!

ELDER YOUNG
DING DONG!

ELDERS
AND IF YOU LET US IN WE'LL SHOW
YOU HOW IT CAN BE DONE!

ELDER GRANT
NO THANKS?

ELDER GREEN
YOU SURE?

ELDER GRANT
OH WELL.

ELDER GREEN
THAT'S FINE.

ELDER GRANT

GOODBYE!

ELDER GREEN

HAVE FUN IN HELL.

ELDER GRANT & ELDER CROSS
Hey now!

ELDERS

YOU SIMPLY WON'T BELIEVE
HOW MUCH THIS BOOK WILL
CHANGE YOUR LIFE,
THIS BOOK WILL CHANGE YOUR LIFE,
THIS BOOK WILL CHANGE YOUR LIFE!
THIS BOOK WILL CHANGE YOUR LIFE!
THIS BOOK WILL CHANGE YOUR LIFE!

*Shy, nerdy ELDER ARNOLD
CUNNINGHAM walks up and with
a big gesture rings a fake doorbell.
DWANG, DONG, DWOONG!!!*

ELDER CUNNINGHAM
Hello?! Would you like to change
religions, I have a free book written
by Jesus!

*Silence. All the Elders glare at
him. Now a big, booming VOICE
comes out of the darkness.*

VOICE
NO, NO, ELDER CUNNINGHAM!
That's NOT how we do it. You're
making things up again. JUST STICK
TO THE APPROVED DIALOGUE.
Elders, show him.

*The music starts again and the
Elders all sing around Arnold,
who tries to keep up.*

ELDERS

HELLO!

ELDER CUNNINGHAM
Hello...

ELDERS

MY NAME IS

ELDER CUNNINGHAM
Elder Cunningham?

ELDERS

AND WE WOULD LIKE TO SHARE
WITH YOU
THIS BOOK OF JESUS CHRIST!

ELDER PRICE

HELLO!

ELDER GRANT

HELLO!

ELDER GREEN

DING DONG!

ELDER WHITE

HEIGH HO!

ELDER SMITH

JUST TAKE THIS BOOK!

ELDER YOUNG

IT'S FREE!

ELDER PRICE

FOR YOU!

ELDER HARRIS

FROM ME!

ELDER GRANT

YOU SEE?

ELDERS

YOU SIMPLY WON'T BELIEVE
HOW MUCH THIS BOOK WILL
CHANGE YOUR LIFE!
HELLO

THIS BOOK WILL CHANGE YOUR LIFE!

HELLO

SO YOU WON'T BURN IN

ELDER WHITE

HEL - LO!

ELDERS

YOU'RE GONNA DIE SOMEDAY!

BUT IF YOU READ THIS BOOK
     YOU'LL SEE
     THAT THERE'S ANOTHER WAY.

SPEND ETERNITY WITH FRIENDS
     AND FAMILY.

WE CAN FULLY GUARANTEE YOU
     THAT

THIS BOOK WILL CHANGE YOUR LIFE.

HELLO!

THIS BOOK WILL CHANGE YOUR LIFE!

HELLO!

THIS BOOK WILL CHANGE YOUR LIFE!

THE BOOK OF MORMON!

MORMON!

HELLO!!!

The same booming voice is heard–

VOICE

Alright, Elders, that was very good indeed. You have been training for three months and you are now...READY TO GO OUT AND SPREAD THE WORD!

The Elders all look at each other and jump around with excitement.

ELDERS

Alright! / Yes! / We graduated! / Etc.

VOICE

In a moment you will be assigned

your mission companions and locations!

More excitement and CHATTER from the Elders.

ELDER PRICE

Oh boy! Oh boy this is IT, guys!

ELDER YOUNG

I can't believe the day is here! We get to go out and see the world!

ELDER SMITH

Do you have any idea where they're sending you, Elder Price?

ELDER PRICE

Well... Of course, we don't REALLY have final say over where we get sent... But I have been PRAYING to be sent to my favorite place in the world...

ELDER GRANT

Well, if YOU prayed for a location I'm sure Heavenly Father will make it happen! You're like the smartest, best, most deserving Elder the center has ever seen!

ELDERS

Yeah! / That's right! / Etc.

ELDER PRICE

Aw, come on guys...

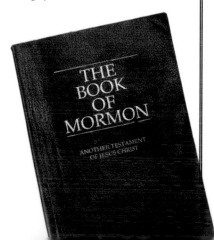

WE CAN FUL[L]
YOU
THIS BO[O]
CHA[
YOU[R]

GUARANTEE
THAT
OK WILL
NGE
R LIFE

The Elders all turn and talk to each other as Price steps forward and addresses the crowd.

TWO BY TWO

ELDER PRICE

> THE MOST IMPORTANT TIME OF
>   A MORMON KID'S LIFE
> IS HIS MISSION.
> A CHANCE TO GO OUT AND HELP
>   HEAL THE WORLD,
> THAT'S MY MISSION.
> SOON I'LL BE OFF IN A DIFFERENT
>   PLACE,
> HELPING THE WHOLE HUMAN
>   RACE.
> I KNOW MY MISSION WILL BE
>   SOMETHING INCREDIBLE.

VOICE
Elders, form a line and step forward when your name is called! Elder Young!

Young runs to center stage.

ELDER YOUNG
Yes, sir!

VOICE
Your mission brother will be... ELDER GRANT!!!

Grant steps out of the crowd.

ELDER GRANT
That's...that's me!

Elder Grant runs out to stand next to Young and they high-five each other.

ELDER GRANT
Hey brother!

They shake hands.

VOICE
And your mission location is... NORWAY!

ELDER YOUNG
Oh wow, NORWAY!

ELDER GRANT
Land of gnomes and trolls!!

ELDER GRANT & ELDER YOUNG

> TWO BY TWO WE'RE MARCHING
>   DOOR TO DOOR!
> 'CAUSE GOD LOVES MORMONS
>   AND HE WANTS SOME MORE!
> A TWO-YEAR MISSION IS OUR
>   SACRIFICE
> WE ARE THE ARMY OF THE
>   CHURCH OF JESUS CHRIST!
> [OF LATTER-DAY SAINTS]

ELDERS

> TWO BY TWO AND TODAY WE'LL
>   KNOW
> WHO WE'LL MAKE THE
>   JOURNEY WITH AND WHERE
>   WE'LL GO.
> WE'RE FIGHTING FOR A CAUSE BUT
>   WE'RE REALLY REALLY NICE,
> WE ARE THE ARMY OF THE
>   CHURCH OF JESUS CHRIST!
> [OF LATTER-DAY SAINTS]

VOICE
Elder White and Elder Smith!

White and Smith now take center stage.

ELDER SMITH
I KNEW we'd get paired together!

VOICE
Your location will be FRANCE!

ELDER WHITE
FRANCE! Land of pastries and
turtlenecks!

ELDER SMITH & ELDER WHITE
TWO BY TWO I GUESS IT'S YOU
AND ME.
WE'RE OFF TO PREACH ACROSS
LAND AND SEA!

ELDER WHITE
Satan has a hold of France!

ELDER SMITH
We need to knock him off his perch!

ELDERS
WE ARE THE SOLDIERS OF THE ARMY
OF THE CHURCH!
[OF JESUS CHRIST OF LATTER-DAY
SAINTS]

VOICE
Elder Cross and Elder Green!

The new two take center stage.

VOICE
You will be serving in JAPAN!

ELDER GREEN
Oh boy, Japan!

ELDER CROSS
Land of soy sauce –

ELDER GREEN
And Mothra!

VOICE
Elder Harris and Elder Brown...

*Now our hero, Elder Price, steps
forward into a spotlight, having a
moment to himself as the action
continues in the dark behind him.*

ELDER PRICE
HEAVENLY FATHER, WHERE WILL I
GO ON MY MISSION?

ELDERS
ON MY MISSION

ELDER PRICE
WILL IT BE CHINA OR OL' MEXICO
ON MY MISSION?

ELDERS
MY MISSION...

ELDER PRICE
IT COULD BE SAN FRAN BY THE BAY,
AUSTRALIA WHERE THEY SAY
"G'DAY!"
(crossing his fingers)
BUT I PRAY I'M SENT TO MY
FAVORITE PLACE –
ORLANDO!

ELDERS
ORLANDO

ELDER PRICE
I LOVE YOU

ELDER PRICE & ELDERS
ORLANDO!

ELDER PRICE
SEA WORLD AND DISNEY AND

ELDER PRICE & ELDERS
PUTT PUTT GOLFING

VOICE
Elder Price!

Price is snapped out of his moment and runs back to center stage.

ELDER PRICE
Yes, sir!!!

VOICE
Your brother will be...ELDER Cunningham!

The nerdy Cunningham comes bouncing out.

ELDER CUNNINGHAM
That's! That's ME!

He struts out to Price and gives a big dorky wave.

ELDER CUNNINGHAM
HELLO!!!

ELDER PRICE
Oh... Hi...

VOICE
And your mission location is... UGANDA!!!!

MUSIC STOPS.

ELDER PRICE
...Uganda?

ELDER CUNNINGHAM
UGANDA! COOL! WHERE IS THAT?!

VOICE
AFRICA!

Price looks visibly upset, but then bucks up and tries to rally himself.

ELDER CUNNINGHAM
Oh BOY– Like *Lion King*!

The other Elders all dance forward, but Price still looks a little shocked.

ELDERS
(Price still perplexed)
> TWO BY TWO –
> AND NOW IT'S TIME TO GO.
> OUR PATHS HAVE BEEN REVEALED
> SO LET'S START THE SHOW!
> OUR SHIRTS ARE CLEANED AND
>   PRESSED
> AND OUR HAIRCUTS ARE PRECISE
> WE ARE THE ARMY OF THE
>   CHURCH,
> WE ARE THE ARMY OF THE
>   CHURCH,
> WE ARE THE ARMY OF THE CHURCH
>   OF JESUS CHRIST!
> [OF LATTER-DAY SAINTS!]

Even through the rest of the song, Price seems a bit confused and is still reeling from not getting sent to Orlando.

ELDERS
> TWO BY TWO
> WE MARCH FOR VICTORY
> ARMED WITH THE GREATEST BOOK
>   IN HISTORY

WE'LL CONVERT EVERYONE ALL
ACROSS THE PLANET EARTH!
THAT IS THE BEAUTY OF
THE ESSENCE OF
THE PURPOSE OF
THE MISSION OF
THE SOLDIERS OF
THE ARMY OF THE CHURCH
OF JESUS CHRIST!
[OF LATTER-DAY SAINTS]

VOICE
Alright Elders, go home and pack
your things! Tomorrow, your
missions begin!

*The other Elders all happily
walk off in their pairs, ad
libbing happy conversation and
patting each other on the back,
leaving Price and Cunningham
alone. Price looks a little
uncomfortable, Cunningham
looks thrilled.*

ELDER CUNNINGHAM
I am SO STOKED we got paired
together Elder Price!

ELDER PRICE
Yeah, so am I. This is...fantastic.

ELDER CUNNINGHAM
You know what? I PRAYED to
Heavenly Father that we would
get paired together. HE REALLY
DOES LISTEN!

ELDER PRICE
(confused)
He ANSWERED your prayer, huh?

ELDER CUNNINGHAM
Yup! My mom always said if
Heavenly Father is proud of you
he'll always give you what you

ask! YOU AND ME, FOR TWO
YEARS IN UGHAN-DAH! THIS IS
GONNA BE AWESOME!!

ELDER PRICE
Yes, I'm sure the Book of Mormon
will do those Africans a lot of good.

ELDER CUNNINGHAM
(laughs in his face)
AHH HA HA HAA!!

*Cunningham realizes he laughed
at the wrong time.*

ELDER CUNNINGHAM
Well, see ya tomorrow, companion.
TOMORROW IS ALWAYS A
LATTER DAY!!!

*Cunningham pounces offstage
and Price is left staring up at his God.*

- SALT LAKE CITY AIRPORT -

*Elder Price and Elder
Cunningham have their
suitcases and are each
surrounded by their families.*

Note that Price's mom is most likely going to have to be played by a male, so we can put a guy in drag and just have him sobbing into a hanky.

PRICE'S DAD
Goodbye, son, we are SO proud of you!

PRICE'S BROTHER
Oh, I can't believe Kevin is going to Africa for TWO YEARS! I'm gonna miss my brother so much!

ELDER PRICE
I know, I'm going to miss you guys, too! Maybe we should see if there's any way I can get assigned somewhere a little closer to home. Like... Florida...or...

PRICE'S DAD
(chuckling)
Ho! Don't worry, son. Heavenly

Father has a hand in everything.
(pointing up)
He knows what's best... He always knows!

ELDER PRICE
You're right, dad... I'm sure I'll have an amazing time.

Now we focus on Cunningham with his family.

CUNNINGHAM'S DAD
Alright, son, remember, just do whatever Elder Price tells you. He is a great Mormon. The kind of kid any parent would be proud of.

ELDER CUNNINGHAM
Right! And I'm a FOLLOWER!

CUNNINGHAM'S DAD
That's right. Do your best. Maybe your new companion can help make you not so weird.

ELDER CUNNINGHAM
Yeah, we're gonna have the most amazing time together! It's like...
(stepping out to audience)
It's like I'm finally gonna have a best friend...

CUNNINGHAM'S DAD
And REMEMBER, Arnold, what we talked about in regards to your... little PROBLEM.

ELDER CUNNINGHAM
Don't worry, dad, my little problem is IN CHECK! Not gonna be an issue!

Price has overheard this–

ELDER PRICE
Uh, what's the – "little problem"?

CUNNINGHAM'S DAD
Our little Arnold can sometimes be…Well… He has a very ACTIVE imagination.

ELDER CUNNINGHAM
I LIE A LOT!

CUNNINGHAM'S DAD
NO! He – he just sometimes MAKES THINGS UP when he doesn't know what to say.

ELDER CUNNINGHAM
Bishop Donahue says it's because I have no self-esteem and desperately want to fit in with my peers!

PRICE'S DAD
Well, alright everyone! I think it's time we leave these two to their work! That's right, you boys have a lot of catching up to do now that you're companions! This is it, Elders. You're heading…TO AFRICA!!!!!

The families make it offstage. The lights go dark and a spot comes up on a Lion King-*like character who enters stage*

LION KING CHARACTER
    HEY NA DA HEY NA! AYA BUBBU
        TAYA TAYAAAAAAAAA!
    HAIYAAAA TAYAAA MALA
        ENNYAAAAA! HEY NAAA NAAA
        NAAA DA HAYAAA!

Finally the lights come up, the families are back, and we are STILL at the airport.

PRICE'S DAD
How did you like THAT, boys?! A

real LION KING SEND-OFF!!! We got Mrs. Brown to sing like an African for you.

ELDER PRICE
That's great dad, thanks.

LION KING CHARACTER
(waving)
Good luck, boys! I've never been to Africa, but I'm sure it's a hoot!

CUNNINGHAM'S DAD
Goodbye, son! Please be careful!

PRICE'S DAD
Get out there and baptize those Africans, boy!

ELDER PRICE
Bye, Mrs. Brown.

MRS. BROWN
Bye, baby.

Mrs. Brown walks off. The families walk off as well. The boys sit down next to each other.

ELDER CUNNINGHAM
Well… It's just you and me now, companion.

ELDER PRICE
Yup, that's right, Elder.

ELDER CUNNINGHAM
From this point on, according to missionary rule number seventy-two we are never to go anywhere without each other, except the bathroom!

ELDER PRICE
Yes, that's right.

ELDER CUNNINGHAM
It's so awesome because my
friends always end up leaving me,
but YOU CAN'T! HA HA HAAA!!

Price looks sad.

ELDER CUNNINGHAM
OKAY! Favorite movies! Are you a
Star Wars guy or a *Star Trek* guy?!
I wanna know EVERYTHING
ABOUT YOU. Personally I like *Star
Wars* but I'm willing to like *Star Trek*
more if YOU think it's better.

*Price stares at him a minute,
then closes his eyes, takes a
breath and tries a new strategy.*

ELDER PRICE
Elder... I like to have fun just as
much as the next guy. But things are
different now, you know?
We're MEN now. This is OUR TIME
to PROVE that we are worthy.

ELDER CUNNINGHAM
Worthy of what?

ELDER PRICE
Of everything we've been promised
in the afterlife...

Slow music starts.

YOU AND ME
(BUT MOSTLY ME)

ELDER PRICE
I'VE ALWAYS HAD THE HOPE,
THAT ON THE DAY I GO TO
HEAVEN,

HEAVENLY FATHER WILL SHAKE
MY HAND AND SAY
"YOU'VE DONE AN AWESOME JOB,
KEVIN,"
NOW IT'S OUR TIME TO GO OUT

ELDER CUNNINGHAM
MY BEST FRIEND

ELDER PRICE
AND SET THE WORLD'S PEOPLE
FREE.
AND WE CAN DO IT TOGETHER,
YOU AND ME,
BUT MOSTLY ME.

*Price takes Cunningham under
his wing.*

ELDER PRICE
YOU AND ME – BUT MOSTLY ME –
ARE GONNA CHANGE THE WORLD
FOREVER.
CUZ I CAN DO MOST ANYTHING!

ELDER CUNNINGHAM
AND I CAN STAND NEXT TO YOU
AND WATCH.

ELDER PRICE
EVERY HERO NEEDS A SIDEKICK –
EVERY CAPTAIN NEEDS A MATE.

ELDER CUNNINGHAM

AYE AYE!

ELDER PRICE

EVERY DINNER NEEDS A SIDE DISH–

ELDER CUNNINGHAM

ON A SLIGHTLY SMALLER PLATE!

BOTH

AND NOW WE'RE SEEING EYE TO
EYE,
IT'S SO GREAT WE CAN AGREE
THAT HEAVENLY FATHER HAS
CHOSEN YOU AND ME

ELDER PRICE

JUST MOSTLY ME!

*Price steps away from
Cunningham, ignoring him
again and leaving him in the
background.*

ELDER PRICE

SOMETHING INCREDIBLE... I'LL DO
SOMETHING INCREDIBLE...
I WANT TO BE THE MORMON WHO
CHANGED ALL OF MANKIND

ELDER CUNNINGHAM

MY BEST FRIEND

ELDER PRICE

IT'S SOMETHING I'VE FORESEEN.
NOW THAT I'M NINETEEN,
I'LL DO SOMETHING INCREDIBLE,
THAT BLOWS GOD'S FREAKING
MIND!

BOTH

AND AS LONG AS WE STICK
TOGETHER

ELDER CUNNINGHAM

AND I STAY OUT OF YOUR WAY

ELDER PRICE

OUT OF MY WAY

BOTH

WE WILL CHANGE THE WORLD
FOREVER

ELDER CUNNINGHAM

AND MAKE TOMORROW A LATTER
DAY!

ELDER PRICE

MOSTLY ME!

BOTH

SO STOP SINGING ABOUT IT, AND DO
IT!
HOW READY AND PSYCHED ARE WE?!
LIFE IS ABOUT TO CHANGE FOR YOU
AND –
LIFE IS ABOUT TO CHANGE
FOR ME AND –
LIFE IS ABOUT TO CHANGE
FOR YOU AND –
ME –

ELDER PRICE

BUT ME MOSTLY.
AND THERE'S NO LIMIT TO
WHAT WE CAN DO –
ME AND YOU.
BUT MOSTLY MEEEEEEE!

- A SMALL VILLAGE IN NORTHERN UGANDA -

*As the boys walk out onto the
stage with their bags, the music
starts to slow down, fall apart
...and finally stop.*

The boys look around in horror

at the poverty they see.

A man walks in front of them dragging a donkey carcass. The boys just watch him pass.

ELDER CUNNINGHAM
Wow! Here we are, huh, buddy?! We made it!

ELDER PRICE
(obviously a little freaked out and grossed out)
Yeah, that was...that was ONE LONG TRIP.

Cunningham takes out his video camera and points it at Price.

ELDER CUNNINGHAM
(narrating for camera)
Here we are, in KIT-GU-LI UGANDA! What'dya think about Uganda, Elder?!

ELDER PRICE
I think it's really DIFFERENT!

ELDER CUNNINGHAM
YEAH!! IT'S DIFFERENT!!!

Two very bad-ass guards with sunglasses and machine guns walk up threateningly to the boys.

GENERAL'S GUARD #1
YA! YA! WHAT WE GOT HERE, MAYBE?! GERMAN?! BRITISH?!

ELDER PRICE
Hello!

GENERAL'S GUARD #1
AMERICAN.

ELDER PRICE
Uh, we are supposed to meet

(reading note)
a mister Mafala Hatimbi.

GENERAL'S GUARD #1
YOUR BAGS!

ELDER PRICE
Oh sure. We don't have anything illegal, sirs.

The guards take the bags, rip them open and start tearing through everything inside.

ELDER PRICE
We are from the Church of Jesus Christ of Latter-Day Saints.

ELDER CUNNINGHAM
(still videotaping)
Here are some men with guns looking through our bags!

GENERAL'S GUARD #2
SHUT UP!

After they finish going through the bags, they close them up again.

GENERAL'S GUARD #2
We take these bags!

ELDER CUNNINGHAM
WHAT?!

GENERAL'S GUARD #1
This is your TARIFF to The General!

ELDER PRICE
The General? HEY WAIT A MINUTE!

Suddenly, the guards PUMP their shotguns and M-16s and shove them in the Elders' faces.

GENERAL'S GUARD #1
YOU SHUT THE FUCK UP YOU WANNA DIE?!

ELDER PRICE
Oh my gosh! Okay! Okay!

ELDER CUNNINGHAM
JUST take the bags! WHY ARE YOU DOING THIS?!

The guards walk away. That's when another Ugandan man, MAFALA HATIMBI, comes walking in happily.

MAFALA
(big and happy)
AHHH! There you are! I have been looking for you! I am Mafala Hatimbi. I've been hired to show you to your building.

ELDER PRICE
Oh, thank goodness! Some men just took our bags!

MAFALA
Oh, yes you must be very careful around here! Now let's get going!

He starts to lead the boys away.

ELDER PRICE
Well, no, first shouldn't we talk to the police about getting our bags back?

MAFALA
The police?! Ha, ha! The police are in Kampala! Two days' drive away!

ELDER PRICE
But a lot of important stuff was in those bags!

MAFALA
Oh well, "Hasa Diga Eebowai!"

ELDER CUNNINGHAM
Excuse me?

HASA DIGA EEBOWAI

MAFALA
You're in NORTHERN Uganda now!

MUSIC kicks in.

MAFALA
And in this part of Africa, we ALL have a saying – whenever something bad happens, we just throw our hands up to the sky and say HASA DIGA EEBOWAI!

ELDER CUNNINGHAM
Hasa Diga Eebowai?

MAFALA
It's the only way to get through all these troubled times. There's war, famine...but having a saying makes it all seem better...

MAFALA
THERE ISN'T ENOUGH FOOD TO EAT.

UGANDANS
HASA DIGA EEBOWAI!

MAFALA
PEOPLE ARE STARVING IN THE STREET.

UGANDANS & MAFALA
HASA DIGA EEBOWAI!
HASA DIGA EEBOWAI!
HASA DIGA EEBOWAI!

ELDER PRICE
Hey, that's pretty neat!

ELDER CUNNINGHAM
Does it mean no worries for the rest of our days?

MAFALA
Kind of!
WE'VE HAD NO RAIN IN SEVERAL DAYS.

UGANDANS
HASA DIGA EEBOWAI!

MAFALA
AND EIGHTY PERCENT OF US HAVE AIDS.

UGANDANS
HASA DIGA EEBOWAI!

MAFALA
MANY YOUNG GIRLS HERE GET CIRCUMCISED,
THEIR CLITS GET CUT RIGHT OFF.

UGANDANS
WAY OH!

WOMEN
AND SO WE SAY UP TO THE SKY:

UGANDANS
HASA DIGA EEBOWAI!
HASA DIGA EEBOWAI!
HASA DIGA EEBOWAI!

MAFALA
Now you try. Just stand up tall, tilt your head to the sky, and list all the bad things in YOUR life.

Elder Cunningham steps up.

ELDER CUNNINGHAM
SOMEBODY TOOK OUR LUGGAGE AWAY!

UGANDANS
HASA DIGA EEBOWAI!

ELDER PRICE
THE PLANE WAS CROWDED AND THE BUS WAS LATE!

UGANDANS
HASA DIGA EEBOWAI!

MAFALA
WHEN THE WORLD IS GETTING YOU DOWN,
THERE'S NOBODY ELSE TO BLAME.

UGANDANS
WAY OH!

MAFALA
RAISE A MIDDLE FINGER TO THE SKY,
AND CURSE HIS ROTTEN NAME.

ELDER PRICE
Wait, what?

Elder Cunningham is out of earshot, jamming with some Ugandans.

UGANDANS & ELDER CUNNINGHAM
HASA DIGA EEBOWAI!

ELDER CUNNINGHAM
Am I saying it right?

UGANDANS
HASA DIGA EEBOWAI!

ELDER PRICE
Excuse me, what EXACTLY does that phrase mean?

MAFALA
Well, let's see…"Eebowai" means "God", and "Hasa Diga" means "FUCK YOU". So I guess in English it would be, "Fuck you, God!"

UGANDANS
HASA DIGA EEBOWAI!

ELDER PRICE
What?!!

MAFALA
WHEN GOD FUCKS YOU IN THE BUTT

UGANDANS
HASA DIGA EEBOWAI!

MAFALA
FUCK GOD BACK RIGHT IN HIS CUNT!

UGANDANS
HASA DIGA EEBOWAI!

ELDER CUNNINGHAM
HASA DIGA EEBOWAI!
WHAT A NIFTY PHRASE!

UGANDANS
WAY OH!

ELDER CUNNINGHAM
HASA DIGA EEBOWAI!
HASA DIGA EEBOWAI!
HASA DIGA EEBOWAI!

(He keeps going –)

HA
DIC
EEBC

SAGA GAWAI!

ELDER PRICE
(overlapping –)
Elder Cunningham. Elder
Cunningham. Stop – Elder
Cunningham. ELDER
CUNNINGHAM!

ELDER CUNNINGHAM
What, what, what?

ELDER PRICE
Don't say that!

ELDER CUNNINGHAM
What? Hasa Diga –

ELDER PRICE
Don't say it! It means something
very bad.

ELDER CUNNINGHAM
What?

ELDER PRICE
They're saying F you to Heavenly
Father!

ELDER CUNNINGHAM
F you Heavenly Father?! Holy Moly!
I said it like thirteen times!

UGANDANS
  HASA DIGA EEBOWAI!
  FUCK YOU, GOD!
  HASA DIGA EEBOWAI!
  FUCK YOU, GOD!

*Price and Cunningham
approach Mafala.*

ELDER PRICE
Sir, you really should not be saying
that. Things aren't always as bad
as they seem.

MAFALA
Oh really? Well, take this fucking
asshole MUTUMBO. He got caught
last week trying to RAPE A BABY.

ELDER PRICE
What? Why?

MAFALA
Some people in his tribe believe
having sex with a virgin can cure
their AIDS. There aren't many
virgins left, so some of them are
turning to babies!

ELDER PRICE
But...but that's HORRIBLE?!

MAFALA
I know!

UGANDANS
  HASA DIGA EEBOWAI!

MAFALA
  HERE'S THE BUTCHER, HE HAS AIDS.
  HERE'S THE TEACHER, SHE HAS AIDS.
  HERE'S THE DOCTOR, HE HAS AIDS –
  HERE'S MY DAUGHTER, SHE HAS A...

They hang on his words...

MAFALA

...WONDERFUL DISPOSITION.

SHE'S ALL I HAVE LEFT IN THE
WORLD.

AND IF EITHER OF YOU LAYS A
HAND ON HER –

I WILL GIVE YOU MY AIDS.

ELDER CUNNINGHAM
No!!!

The Ugandans laugh and party.

UGANDANS

IF YOU DON'T LIKE WHAT WE SAY
TRY LIVING HERE A COUPLE DAYS.

WATCH ALL YOUR FRIENDS AND
FAMILY DIE.

HASA DIGA EEBOWAI! FUCK YOU!

HASA DIGA EEBOWAI!

FUCK YOU GOD IN THE ASS, MOUTH,
AND CUNT-A,

FUCK YOU GOD IN THE ASS, MOUTH,
AND CUNT-A,

FUCK YOU GOD IN THE ASS, MOUTH,
AND CUNT-A,

FUCK YOU IN THE EYE.

HASA –

DIGA EEBOWAI

HASA –

FUCK YOU IN THE OTHER EYE.

HASA DIGA EEBOWAI!

HASA DIGA EEBOWAI!

FUCK YOU,

FUCK YOU GOD!

FUCK YOU,

FUCK YOU GOD!

HASA DIGA,

FUCK YOU GOD!

IN THE CUNT!

After the inevitable thunderous

applause, we can start the music
up again as the set changes and
MAFALA'S DAUGHTER leads
the boys as if walking them
down some village street.*

- MORMON
MISSIONARIES'
LIVING QUARTERS -

*The daughter leads the two boys
up to the very small and humble
little apartment building. Price
is still in a bit of a daze from
what he heard the Ugandans
singing.*

NABULUNGI
This is where my father asked me
to bring you. The others like you
should be inside.

ELDER CUNNINGHAM
Thank you so much, Jon Bon Jovi.

NABULUNGI
Nabulungi.

ELDER CUNNINGHAM
Nab... Bon Jovi.

ELDER PRICE
I'm sorry, we appreciate your
help, Nabulungi. Look, uh, maybe
sometime, Elder Cunningham and I
could talk to you about things. Sort
of tell you a little about the Church
of Jesus Christ of Latter-Day Saints.

*Cunningham again realizes he
has laughed inappropriately.*

NABULUNGI
I have to get back to the village. But
I am always there – if you want to
talk to me.

She turns to go but then turns back.

NABULUNGI
Just one piece of advice. No matter how hot you get at night, keep your windows closed. It is the only way to protect against the scorpions... And the mosquitoes. And the Lions. And the murderers and the robbers and the AIDS and the snakes and the safari ants which can actually plant their eggs under your skin and eat you from the inside out.

She walks away. Cunningham stares after her but Price turns away and wipes his forehead.

ELDER PRICE
(big sigh, wipes his brow)
Oh man, Elder, can you believe this?

ELDER CUNNINGHAM
I know, right... She is such a hot shade of black. She's like a latte.

ELDER PRICE
Let's just go inside and meet the other missionaries, alright?

The two walk in the mission door and find an empty room inside the living quarters.

ELDER PRICE
Hello?

Suddenly, six bright crisp white Elders jump out from various positions.

ELDER MCKINLEY
The new recruits are here!

ALL ELDERS
(way too excited)

Oh boy!!!! / Yeah!!! / Alright! / Etc.

ELDER MCKINLEY
WELCOME, Elder Price and Elder Cunningham! I am Elder McKinley, current district leader for this area of the Uganda Mission.

ELDER PRICE
Great to meet you.

ELDER CHURCH
My name is Elder Church. Originally from the great city of Cheyenne, Wyoming!

ELDER MICHAELS
Elder Michaels. From Provo.

ELDER THOMAS
Elder Thomas! But the Elders here all call me Elder Pop Tarts because I love 'em so much!

ELDER MCKINLEY
And that's Elder Neeley and Elder Davis.

ELDER CUNNINGHAM
Whew! That's a lot to remember!

ELDERS
(cheesy laughter)

After all the laughter has died out, Cunningham finally chimes in with a badly timed laugh of his own.

ELDER MCKINLEY
Sit, please.

ELDER PRICE
Thank you.

They sit and there is an awkward pause.

ELDER MCKINLEY
Well! We've all been here about three months now. Spreading the word of Christ, and saving the souls of the fine Ugandan people through baptism.

ELDER PRICE
How many have you baptized so far?

ELDER MCKINLEY
Uhhh...zero.

Everyone looks a little ashamed.

ELDERS
Yeah, zero. / Zip. / None, yeah. / Etc.

ELDER CUNNINGHAM
That's practically nothing...

ELDER PRICE
(stands and walks away)
Oh boy...

ELDER CUNNINGHAM
(follows Price)
Hey, you alright, partner?

ELDER PRICE
Yeah, I'm just a little CONFUSED right now, okay?

ELDERS
Oooooh, confuuused!! / Confused, yeah... / Etc.

ELDER MCKINLEY
Well, Elder, that is NATURAL. There are certainly a lot of things here in Uganda that can be... disturbing. But your mission has officially started, which means you need to do what WE have all done...

TURN IT OFF

ELDER MCKINLEY
I'VE GOT A FEELIN',
    THAT YOU COULD BE FEELIN' –
A WHOLE LOT BETTER THAN YOU
    FEEL TODAY.
YOU SAY YOU'VE GOT A PROBLEM?
WELL THAT'S NO PROBLEM,
IT'S SUPER EASY NOT TO FEEL THAT
    WAY.
WHEN YOU START TO GET
    CONFUSED
BECAUSE OF THOUGHTS IN YOUR
    HEAD –
DON'T FEEL THOSE FEELINGS –
HOLD THEM IN – IN – STEAD!
TURN 'EM OFF!
LIKE A LIGHT SWITCH,
JUST GO "CLICK"
IT'S A COOL LITTLE MORMON TRICK.
WE DO IT ALL THE TIME.
WHEN YOU'RE FEELING CERTAIN
    FEELINGS
THAT JUST DON'T SEEM RIGHT,

TREAT THOSE PESKY FEELINGS LIKE A
READING LIGHT

ELDER MICHAELS
AND TURN 'EM OFF!
LIKE A LIGHT SWITCH!

ELDER CHURCH
JUST GO BAP!

ELDER NEELEY
REALLY, WHAT'S SO HARD ABOUT
THAT?

ELDER MCKINLEY
TURN IT OFF!

ALL ELDERS
TURN IT OFF!

*Now another Elder steps in to
sing. This whole time, Price
looks confused and Cunningham
seems to be enjoying himself.*

ELDER CHURCH
WHEN I WAS YOUNG, MY DAD
WOULD TREAT MY MOM
REAL BAD
EVERY TIME THE UTAH JAZZ
WOULD LOSE.
HE'D START A'DRINKIN' AND I'D
START A'THINKIN'
HOW'M I GONNA KEEP MY MOM
FROM GETTING ABUSED?

I'D SEE HER ALL SCARED AND MY
SOUL WAS DYIN'!
MY DAD WOULD SAY TO ME,
"NOW DON'T YOU DARE START
CRYIN'!"
TURN IT OFF!

ELDERS
LIKE A LIGHT SWITCH.
JUST GO FLICK!
IT'S OUR NIFTY LITTLE MORMON
TRICK!

ELDER CHURCH
TURN IT OFF!

ELDERS
TURN. IT. OFF!

ELDER THOMAS
MY SISTER WAS A DANCER
BUT SHE GOT CANCER.
THE DOCTOR SAID SHE STILL HAD
TWO MONTHS MORE.
I THOUGHT SHE HAD TIME,
SO I GOT IN LINE FOR THE
NEW iPHONE AT THE APPLE STORE.
SHE LAID THERE DYING WITH
MY FATHER AND MOTHER.
HER VERY LAST WORDS WERE
'WHERE IS MY BROTHER?'

ELDERS
TURN IT OFF!

ELDER THOMAS
YEAH!

ELDERS
BID THOSE SAD FEELINGS ADIEU!

ELDER THOMAS
THE FEAR THAT I MIGHT GET
CANCER, TOO.

ELDER MCKINLEY

> WHEN I WAS IN FIFTH GRADE,
> I HAD A FRIEND, STEVE BLADE –

ELDERS

> STEVE BLADE

ELDER MCKINLEY

> HE AND I WERE CLOSE AS TWO
> FRIENDS COULD BE.

ELDERS

> WE COULD BE CLOSE OOOH

ELDER MCKINLEY

> ONE THING LED TO ANOTHER,
> AND SOON I WOULD DISCOVER

ELDERS

> WOW

ELDER MCKINLEY

> I WAS HAVING REALLY STRANGE
> FEELINGS FOR STEVE.

ELDERS

> FEELINGS FOR STEVE

ELDER MCKINLEY

> I THOUGHT ABOUT US ON A
> DESERTED ISLAND,

ELDERS

> WE'RE ALL ALONE

ELDER MCKINLEY

> WE'D SWIM NAKED IN THE SEA
> AND THEN HE'D TRY AND –
> WHOA! TURN IT OFF!
> LIKE A LIGHT SWITCH.
> THERE, IT'S GONE.

ELDER CHURCH
Good for you!

ELDER MCKINLEY

> MY HETERO SIDE JUST WON.
> I'M ALL BETTER NOW.
> BOYS SHOULD BE WITH GIRLS,
>   THAT'S HEAVENLY FATHER'S
>   PLAN.
> SO IF YOU EVER FEEL YOU'D RATHER
>   BE WITH A MAN –
> TURN IT OFF.

ELDER PRICE
Well, Elder McKinley, I think it's
okay to have gay thoughts. So long
as you never act upon them.

ELDER MCKINLEY
No,

> BECAUSE THEN YOU'RE JUST
>   KEEPING IT DOWN.
> LIKE A DIMMER SWITCH ON LOW...

ELDERS

> ON LOW

ELDER MCKINLEY

> THINKING NOBODY NEEDS TO KNOW.

ELDERS

> UH-OH

TURN
LIKE A LIG
JUS
CLI

T OFF.
T SWITCH.
GO
CK

ELDER MCKINLEY

> BUT THAT'S NOT TRUE.
> BEING GAY IS BAD BUT LYING IS
> WORSE.
> SO JUST REALIZE YOU HAVE A
> CURABLE CURSE –
> AND TURN IT OFF.
> TURN IT OFF.
> TURN IT OFF.
> TURN IT OFF!

There is a short tap dance break.

ELDERS

> TURN IT OFF!

ELDER MCKINLEY
Now how do you feel?

ELDER PRICE
The same.

ELDER MCKINLEY

> THEN YOU'VE ONLY GOT YOURSELF
> TO BLAME.
> YOU DIDN'T PRETEND HARD
> ENOUGH.
> IMAGINE THAT YOUR BRAIN IS
> MADE OF TINY BOXES
> THEN FIND THE BOX THAT'S GAY
> AND CRUSH IT!!

Okay...

ELDER PRICE
Wait...I'm not having gay
thoughts!!!!!

ELDER CUNNINGHAM
Alright! It worked!

ELDERS
Hurray!!!

ELDERS

> HE TURNED IT OFF
> TURN IT OFF

> TURN IT OFF
> TURN IT OFF
> TURN IT OFF
> TURN IT OFF
> LIKE A LIGHTSWITCH
> JUST GO CLICK
> CLICK, CLICK
> WHAT A COOL LITTLE MORMON
> TRICK.
> TRICK, TRICK
> WE DO IT ALL THE TIME.

ELDER MCKINLEY

> WHEN YOU'RE FEELIN'
> CERTAIN FEELINGS THAT JUST
> DON'T SEEM RIGHT,

ELDERS

> DON'T SEEM RIGHT

ELDER MCKINLEY

> TREAT THOSE PESKY FEELINGS
> LIKE A READING LIGHT

ELDERS

> READING LIGHT

ELDER MCKINLEY

> AND TURN 'EM OFFFFFFFF!

ELDERS

> LIKE A LIGHT SWITCH ON A
> CORD
> NOW HE ISN'T GAY ANY...
> TURN IT TURN IT TURN IT TURN IT
> TURN IT TURN IT TURN IT TURN IT
> TUUUUUURN IT

ELDER MCKINLEY

> TURN IT OFF!

ELDERS

> OFFFFFFF!!!!!!

ELDERS
Alright! / Yeah! / Great job, guys! /
Etc.

ELDER MCKINLEY
(quieting them down)
Alright, Elders, alright – our
two new missionaries must be
EXHAUSTED from all their travels.
Let's show them their room. A SIX,
SEVEN, EIGHT!

The Elders all exit.

*Price and Cunningham are
brought into their tiny room,
where two humble beds are
RIGHT NEXT to each other.
Price looks surprised but
Cunningham LEAPS onto
his bed, sits down, and starts
jumping up and down on it.*

ELDER CUNNINGHAM
ALRIGHT! CHECK THIS OUT!!
WE GETTA SLEEP RIGHT NEXT
TO EACH OTHER!!!

ELDER MCKINLEY
Get settled in, Elders. According
to the missionary rules, lights out
promptly at ten and we all wake UP
at exactly 6:30. We've heard a lot of
great things about you, Elder Price.
Really hoping you can turn things
around here.

ELDER CUNNINGHAM
Oh we will!

ELDER MCKINLEY
Elders... We're glad you're here.

*McKinley closes the door, and
walks away.*

ELDER PRICE
ZERO baptisms? This is going to
be a WHOLE LOT harder than we
thought, huh?

ELDER CUNNINGHAM
Yeah! I can see this is gonna be a
LOT like *Lord of the Rings*! You're
Frodo and I'm Samwise fighting
against impossible odds!

ELDER PRICE
This just all isn't what I was
expecting. I've gotta admit, I'm
really starting to feel... I don't
wanna say "ripped off" but just...
overwhelmed.

ELDER CUNNINGHAM
Well, I've got something to admit,
too... Remember when I told you
that I sometimes make things
up, and Bishop Donahue said it's
because I have no self-esteem?

ELDER PRICE
Yeah?

ELDER CUNNINGHAM
It's not true. There is no Bishop
Donahue. I made him up.

Elder Price looks very confused.

ELDER PRICE
Elder, I really think you should just
think about the big day we have
ahead tomorrow, okay? Remember
why we are here. Can you do that
for me?

ELDER CUNNINGHAM
I would do anything for you – I'm
your best friend.

ELDER PRICE
Alright, let's get to sleep.

ELDER CUNNINGHAM
Yeah!

The two boys get into their tiny beds and pull up the sheets. Cunningham happily watches Price as Price just rolls over and pulls the blanket around him. After a while, Elder Cunningham leans over and gently starts to sing.

I AM HERE FOR YOU

ELDER CUNNINGHAM
(singing gently)
> SLEEP NOW LITTLE BUDDY,
> PUT YOUR CARES AWAY.
> NAPPY WITH A HAPPY FACE,
> TOMORROW'S A LATTER DAY

Elder Price's eyes open.

ELDER PRICE
What are you doing?

ELDER CUNNINGHAM
That's what my mom used to sing to make ME feel better.

ELDER PRICE
I feel FINE. But our focus needs to be on our WORK now, Elder. Do you understand how difficult this is going to be? The missionaries here have yet to bring a SINGLE PERSON to the church.

ELDER CUNNINGHAM
Well, if they had already baptized a bunch of Africans here, then it wouldn't be so incredible when

YOU did it, now would it?

Price looks at Cunningham and smiles.

ELDER PRICE
I guess...I guess that's kind of true...

ELDER CUNNINGHAM
Don't forget what you told me, Elder. You are AWESOME. Together we're gonna bring lots of Africans to the church. And then my dad will finally feel proud of me – instead of just feeling "stuck" with me...

ELDER PRICE
You know what, Elder? I think he's got plenty to be proud of already.

ELDER CUNNINGHAM
Really?!

ELDER PRICE
Yeah.

ELDER CUNNINGHAM
> EVENING STAR SHINES BRIGHTLY.
> GOD MAKES LIFE ANEW!
> TOMORROW IS A LATTER DAY
> AND I AM HERE FOR YOU.

ELDER PRICE
> I AM HERE FOR YOU, TOO.

BOTH
> WE ARE HERE
> FOR US.

ELDER CUNNINGHAM
Good night, best friend.

ELDER PRICE
Good night, PAL.

Cunningham takes the blanket from Price.

{ 32 }

- THE VILLAGE -

The people of the village are milling about, working as they sing.

UGANDANS
> HEY NAH HEYY AHH... HAYAAAA...

Nabulungi is happily returning home. She is carrying a large, clunky old typewriter and looking at it like a new prize.

MAFALA
Nabulungi! Where have you been?!

NABULUNGI
Baba! Look what I got at the market!

MAFALA
What have I told you about wandering off?! The market is NOT SAFE!

NABULUNGI
But, Baba, I finally found one! A TEXTING device! Now I can text all my friends!

MAFALA
Listen to me! Do not go to the market again! The General is MUTILATING girls in the next village over!

NABULUNGI
I'm sorry, Baba...

MAFALA
Nabulungi, if we want to stay alive our village needs to LAY LOW and not attract any attention.

On the other side of the stage, closer to some of the houses, the two Mormons happily march in holding their Books of Mormon.

**ELDER PRICE &
ELDER CUNNINGHAM**
> TWO BY TWO WE MARCH FROM
> DOOR TO DOOR!
> CUZ GOD LOVES MORMONS AND HE
> WANTS SOME MORE!

ELDER PRICE
Okay, let's try and get some placements.

ELDER CUNNINGHAM
Right! What's a placement again?

ELDER PRICE
Look, just... Let ME do the talking, alright? You just sort of...SUPPORT what I'm talking about by going "Oh wow" and stuff like that.

ELDER CUNNINGHAM
Oh, yeah! Like the lady in INFOMERCIALS that always says, "Wow, what an incredible offer!" I'm like THAT lady!

ELDER PRICE
Okay fine. Whatever. Why don't we try this little house. Just walk up and do it like at the missionary training center.

ELDER CUNNINGHAM
Okay!

Cunningham looks all around the door.

ELDER CUNNINGHAM
OH NO!!! There's no doorbell!

ELDER PRICE
What?

ELDER CUNNINGHAM
(freaking out)
THEY'VE GOT NO
DOORBELLS!!! WHAT DO WE
DO WHAT DO WE DO!?!?!?

ELDER PRICE
CALM DOWN!

*A Ugandan woman, Kalimba,
comes out the door.*

ELDER PRICE
Oh hello, ma'am! Have you ever felt
that there's an emptiness in your life?

*Kalimba looks around as if to
say, "What the fuck are you
talking about?"*

KALIMBA
What?

ELDER PRICE
When you go to sleep at night
do you sometimes feel a power
STIRRING inside you?

*A Ugandan man in the
background raises his arm and
takes a step forward.*

GOTSWANA
Yes! That's how I feel!

ELDER PRICE
Alright YOU, sir! Step on up here!

*Gotswana steps up to Price as
some other Ugandan people start
to gather around. Price puts his
arm around the man.*

ELDER PRICE
Do you find yourself asking
questions about that strange feeling
inside?

GOTSWANA
YES!

ELDER PRICE
And it's because you want to believe
in something more, isn't it?!

GOTSWANA
No, it's because I have maggots in
my scrotum.

ELDER CUNNINGHAM
YOU'VE GOT WHAT?!

GOTSWANA
I have maggots in my scrotum! You
can help?

ELDER PRICE
Wul, no you should probably see a
doctor.

GOTSWANA
I AM the doctor.

ELDER PRICE
Uh... Yes... Ladies and gentlemen.
We would like to tell you ALL
about a VERY SPECIAL BOOK!
A book that tells you how to find
PARADISE. Through Christ!

UGANDANS
(they've heard this before)
Awww...

*Now Nabulungi enters, arms
folded.*

NABULUNGI
They've HEARD of the Bible. We
ALL have.

ELDER CUNNINGHAM
Bon Bon Jovi! Hey girl.

NABULUNGI
People come and tell us about Jesus and him dying for our sins once a year!

KALIMBA
They always come, tell us the story and then leave. And nothing gets better. Your BIBLE doesn't work.

ELDER PRICE
Of COURSE it didn't work. Those were CHRISTIAN missionaries. We're MORMONS.

NABULUNGI
What's the difference?

ALL-AMERICAN PROPHET

ELDER PRICE
> YOU ALL KNOW THE BIBLE IS MADE
>   OF TESTAMENTS OLD AND NEW.
> YOU'VE BEEN TOLD IT'S JUST THOSE
>   TWO PARTS,
> OR ONLY ONE IF YOU'RE A JEW.
> BUT WHAT IF I WERE TO TELL YOU
> THERE'S A FRESH THIRD PART OUT
>   THERE
> WHICH WAS FOUND BY A HIP NEW
>   PROPHET
> WHO HAD A LITTLE
>   DONNY OSMOND FLAIR...

Price does a flashy Osmond-style dance.

ELDER CUNNINGHAM
(impressed)
Woo hoo!!

ELDER PRICE
> HAVE YOU HEARD OF THE ALL-
>   AMERICAN PROPHET,
> THE BLONDE-HAIRED, BLUE-EYED
>   VOICE OF GOD?
> HE DIDN'T COME FROM THE
>   MIDDLE EAST,
> LIKE THOSE OTHER HOLY MEN;
> NO, GOD'S FAVORITE PROPHET WAS
>   ALL-AMERICAN

I'm gonna take you back to Biblical times, 1823. An American man named Joe livin' on a farm in the Holy Land of Rochester, New York!

Cunningham steps forward like he's doing an infomercial, over-acting and supporting Price.

ELDER CUNNINGHAM
You mean the Mormon prophet Joseph Smith?

ELDER PRICE
That's right, that young man spoke to God.

ELDER CUNNINGHAM
He spoke to God?

ELDER PRICE
And God said, "Joe, people really need to know that the Bible isn't two parts. There's a part three to the Bible, Joe! And I, God, have anointed you to dig up this part three, which is buried by a tree on the hill in your backyard."

ELDER CUNNINGHAM
Wow, God says, "Go to your backyard and start digging"? That makes perfect sense!

ELDER PRICE

> JOSEPH SMITH WENT UP ON THAT
> HILL
> AND DUG WHERE HE WAS TOLD!
> DEEP IN THE GROUND JOSEPH
> FOUND
> SHINING PLATES OF GOLD!

JOSEPH SMITH

What are these golden plates? Who buried them here, and why?

ELDER PRICE

> THEN APPEARED AN ANGEL.
> HIS NAME WAS MORO-NI!

MORONI

I am Moroni

> THE ALL-AMERICAN ANGEL
> MY PEOPLE LIVED HERE LONG,
> LONG AGO!
> THIS IS A HISTORY OF MY RACE
> PLEASE READ THE WORDS WITHIN
> WE WERE JEWS WHO MET WITH
> CHRIST.
> BUT WE WERE ALL-AMERICAN
>
> BUT DON'T LET ANYBODY SEE
> THESE PLATES EXCEPT FOR YOU.
> THEY ARE ONLY FOR YOU TO SEE.
> EVEN IF PEOPLE ASK YOU TO SHOW
> THE PLATES TO THEM,
> DON'T.

JUST COPY THEM ONTO NORMAL
PAPER.
EVEN THOUGH THIS MIGHT MAKE
THEM QUESTION
IF THE PLATES ARE REAL OR NOT.
THIS IS SORT OF WHAT GOD IS
GOING FOR.

ELDER PRICE

> JOSEPH TOOK THE PLATES HOME
> AND WROTE DOWN WHAT HE
> FOUND INSIDE.
> HE TURNED THOSE PLATES INTO A
> BOOK
> THEN RUSHED INTO TOWN AND
> CRIED:

JOSEPH SMITH

> HEY, GOD SPOKE TO ME
> AND GAVE ME THIS BLESSED
> ANCIENT TOME.
> HE HATH COMMANDED ME TO
> PUBLISH IT
> AND STICK IT IN EV'RY HOME

ELDER CUNNINGHAM

Wow! So the Bible is actually a trilogy, and Book of Mormon is *Return of the Jedi*?! I'M interested!

ELDER PRICE

Now, many people didn't believe the prophet Joseph Smith. They thought he'd made up this part three that was buried by a tree on a hill in his backyard.

MORMONS

Liar!

ELDER PRICE

> SO JOE SAID,

JOSEPH SMITH

> THIS IS NO LIE,

I SPEAK TO GOD ALL THE TIME
AND HE'S TOLD ME TO HEAD WEST!
SO I'LL TAKE MY PART THREE
    FROM THE HILL WITH THE TREE,
FEEL FREE IF YOU'D LIKE TO COME
    ALONG WITH ME,
TO THE PROMISED LAND!

MORMONS
The PROMISED LAND?

JOSEPH SMITH
Paradise! On the west coast,
    NOTHING BUT FRUIT AND FIELDS
    AS FAR AS THE EYE CAN SEE!

ALL
HAVE YOU HEARD OF
THE ALL-AMERICAN PROPHET?
HE FOUND A BRAND NEW BOOK
    ABOUT JESUS CHRIST?
WE'RE FOLLOWING HIM TO
    PARADISE,
WE CALL OURSELVES MORMEN,
AND OUR NEW RELIGION IS –
    ALL-AMERICAN.

ELDER CUNNINGHAM
Wow! How much does this all cost?!

ELDER PRICE
THE MORMONS KEPT ON SEARCHING
    FOR THAT PLACE TO SETTLE DOWN
BUT EV'RY TIME THEY THOUGHT
    THEY FOUND IT
THEY GOT KICKED OUT OF TOWN
AND EVEN THOUGH PEOPLE
    WANTED
TO SEE THE GOLDEN PLATES
JOSEPH NEVER SHOWED 'EM!

GOTSWANA
I HAVE MAGGOTS IN MY SCROTUM

The song comes to a halt as Price stares at the man.

ELDER PRICE
Okay – anyway...

ELDER PRICE
NOW COMES THE PART OF OUR
    STORY
    THAT GETS A LITTLE BIT SAD.
ON THE WAY TO THE PROMISED
    LAND,
    MORMONS MADE PEOPLE MAD.
JOSEPH WAS SHOT BY AN ANGRY
    MOB
AND KNEW HE'D SOON BE DONE

TOWNSPEOPLE
OOOOOO –
OOOO –
WAHH
SOON BE DONE

JOSEPH SMITH
YOU MUST LEAD THE PEOPLE NOW
MY GOOD FRIEND BRIGHAM
    YOUNG.

Joseph Smith is left alone to die.

JOSEPH SMITH
OH GOD WHY ARE YOU LETTING
    ME DIE
WITHOUT HAVING ME SHOW
    PEOPLE THE PLATES?
THEY'LL HAVE NO PROOF
    I WAS TELLING THE TRUTH OR
    NOT
THEY'LL HAVE TO BELIEVE IT JUST
    CUZ
OH. I GUESS THAT'S KIND OF WHAT
    YOU WERE GOING FOR.
BLARGGGH

WE CALL O
MORMEN
NE
RELIGIO
AMEI

URSELVES
AND OUR
W
N IS ALL-
RICAN.

ELDER PRICE

The Prophet Joseph Smith died for what he believed in. But his followers, they kept heading west. And Brigham Young led them to Paradise. A sparkling land in Utah they named SALT LAKE CITY. And there the Mormons multiplied! And made big Mormon families!! Generation to generation until finally... They made me!!! And now it's my job to lead you where those early settlers were led so long ago!!!!

TOWNSPEOPLE & ELDER CUNNINGHAM

HOOOOOO –

HOOOO –

AHH

The imaginary pioneers gather around Price.

MORMONS

HAVE YOU HEARD OF THE ALL - AMERICAN PROPHET?

ELDER CUNNINGHAM

Kevin Price!!!

MORMONS

THE NEXT IN LINE TO BE THE VOICE OF GOD?!

ELDER PRICE

My best friend!

MORMONS

HE'S GONNA DO SOMETHING INCREDIBLE!

AND BE JOSEPH SMITH A-GAIN!

CUZ KEVIN PRICE THE PROPHET IS ALL, ALL, ALL, ALL, ALL-AMERICAN!

ELDER CUNNINGHAM

And if you order now, we'll also throw in a set of steak knives!

MORMONS

ALL-AMERICAN!

ELDER PRICE

Alright, now who would like their very own copy of the Book of Mormon?!

UGANDAN WOMAN

What the fuck is a steak knife?

All the Ugandan people look at each other for a beat– and then walk away making groans and making "blow off" gestures with their hands. As they all leave, Nabulungi is obviously hesitating and intrigued.

ELDER PRICE

What were you DOING?!

ELDER CUNNINGHAM

Just doing my part! You know, cuz we're supposed to be a team.

ELDER PRICE

There's nothing in the Book of Mormon about STEAK KNIVES!

ELDER CUNNINGHAM

I'm sorry. I actually never read it.

ELDER PRICE

YOU WHAT?!

ELDER CUNNINGHAM

It's just so boring!

THE GENERAL

JUMAMOSI!!!!!

UGANDANS
(shouts and screams)

SADAKA
(frightened)
He's here! THE GENERAL! HE'S
HERE!!

In a big entrance, we see the
guards from before, and then
The GENERAL breaks through
with OMINOUS MUSIC.

THE GENERAL
What is THIS? Some kind of party?!
Who didn't invite me?!

Everyone cowers and keeps their
heads down. The General walks
over to the boys and looks them
up and down.

THE GENERAL
My NAME...is GENERAL BUTT-
FUCKING NAKED. Because when
I KILL...AND DRINK BLOOD
FOR POWER – I DO IT BUTT-
FUCKING NAKED!!!! This village
belongs to ME.

UGANDAN MAN
We don't belong to anyone! You only
lead a gang of THUGS who mutilate
women for no reason!

THE GENERAL
For no REASON?! The CLITORIS
is an ABOMINATION! Its wicked
pleasure for women has brought a
WRATH UPON UGANDA AND
IT MUST BE CAST OUT!

Nabulungi looks at him, scared.

UGANDAN MAN
My wife's body is none of your
business! And YOU are no general.

The General, walks over to the
man –

THE GENERAL
By the end of the week ALL
females in this village WILL BE
CIRCUMCISED. OR I WILL GET
BUTT-FUCKING NAKED AND
DO THIS!!!

– and shoots the man in the
face. A very realistic and large
squib blows blood and brain
matter all over Elder Price. All
the villagers scream and run
away. Mafala grabs Nabulungi
and pulls her out.

- NABULUNGI'S HOUSE -

Mafala rushes Nabulungi inside.

MAFALA
Alright, I think he's gone. You
have to stay indoors, Nabulungi!
Keep the light off and the windows
closed!

NABULUNGI
No, Baba, I don't want to spend
another night hiding under my bed!

MAFALA
It is the world we live in! We don't
have a choice!

NABULUNGI
Baba – Baba, the white boys! They
said they know the answers to our
problems!

MAFALA
I have to check on the others –

NABULUNGI
LISTEN TO ME, BABA! The
Mormon boys talked about people

who were miserable like us, but they all found somewhere to GO! Somewhere WONDERFUL!
(picking up her typewriter)
I'm going to text them right now and tell them we are interested!

MAFALA
(taking the typewriter from her)
PUT THAT STUPID THING DOWN!
(he sets it down)
JUST STAY INSIDE AND DO NOT OPEN THE DOOR FOR ANYONE!

Her father runs out, slamming the door. She is left alone.

She can hear more SCREAMING coming from the distance outside. She picks up her typewriter again, and looks at it sadly.

Music starts.

SAL TLAY KA SITI

NABULUNGI
MY MOTHER ONCE TOLD ME
    OF A PLACE WITH WATERFALLS
    AND UNICORNS FLYING
WHERE THERE WAS NO SUFFERING,
    NO PAIN
WHERE THERE WAS LAUGHTER
    INSTEAD OF DYING.

I ALWAYS THOUGHT SHE'D MADE IT
    UP
    TO COMFORT ME IN TIMES OF PAIN.
NOW I KNOW THAT PLACE IS REAL.
NOW I KNOW ITS NAME.

SAL TLAY KA SITI,
    JUST LIKE A STORY MAMA TOLD
A VILLAGE IN OOH-TAH,
WHERE THE ROOFS ARE THATCHED
    WITH GOLD.
IF I COULD LET MYSELF BELIEVE,
I KNOW JUST WHERE I'D BE
RIGHT ON THE NEXT BUS TO
    PARADISE.
SAL TLAY KA SITI.

I CAN IMAGINE WHAT IT MUST BE
    LIKE,
THIS PERFECT HAPPY PLACE.
I BET THE GOAT MEAT THERE IS
    PLENTIFUL
AND THEY HAVE VITAMIN
    INJECTIONS BY THE CASE.
THE WARLORDS THERE ARE
    FRIENDLY.
THEY'D HELP YOU CROSS THE
    STREET.
AND THERE'S A RED CROSS ON
    EVERY CORNER
WITH ALL THE FLOUR YOU CAN
    EAT.

SAL TLAY KA SITI,
THE MOST PERFECT PLACE ON
    EARTH.
WHERE FLIES DON'T BITE YOUR
    EYEBALLS
AND HUMAN LIFE HAS WORTH.
IT ISN'T A PLACE OF FAIRY TALES.
IT'S AS REAL AS IT CAN BE.
A LAND WHERE EVIL DOESN'T
    EXIST.
SAL TLAY KA SITI.

AND I'LL BET THE PEOPLE ARE OPEN-
    MINDED,
AND DON'T CARE WHO YOU'VE
    BEEN

AND ALL I HOPE IS THAT WHEN I
    FIND IT,
I'M ABLE TO FIT IN.
WILL I FIT IN?
SAL TLAY KA SITI,
A LAND OF HOPE AND JOY.
AND IF I WANT TO GET THERE,
I JUST HAVE TO FOLLOW THAT
    WHITE BOY.
YOU WERE RIGHT, MAMA,
    YOU DIDN'T LIE.
THIS PLACE IS REAL, AND I'M
    GONNA FLY.

I'M ON MY WAY.
SOON LIFE WON'T BE SO SHITTY.
NOW SALVATION HAS A NAME
SAL TLAY KA... SITI.

*The scene fades down on her
looking outwards longingly.*

- MORMON MISSIONARIES'
LIVING QUARTERS -

*The Elders are studying
scripture. Elder McKinley rushes
in, freaking out.*

ELDER MCKINLEY
O-M GOSH, you guys! I AM
FREAKING OUT!!!

ELDER DAVIS
What is it?

ELDER MCKINLEY
I just got off the phone with the
District Leader. The MISSION
PRESIDENT wants a WRITTEN
PROGRESS REPORT from us THIS
WEEK!!!!

ELDER MICHAELS
A progress report?! But we don't

have any baptisms!!!!

ELDER MCKINLEY
I KNOW THAT! WHAT ARE WE
GONNA DO?!

ELDERS
We're gonna look like failures! / This
is terrible! / Oh gosh, oh no! / My
dad's gonna beat me! / Etc.

ELDER CHURCH
Okay, okay, HOLD ON! I mean...
We COULD...SAY that we had some
baptisms.

The other Elders stare at him.

ELDER MCKINLEY
What, you mean LIE?!

ELDER CHURCH
Well, just sort of.

ELDER SCHRADER
Are you an IDIOT?! MORMONS
don't LIE!

ELDERS
Yeah! / That's right! / Etc.

ELDER NEELEY
I told a lie once when I was twelve,
and I had a dream that I went to
hell! It was REALLY SPOOKY.

ELDER THOMAS
You, too?! I had the hell dream after
I accidentally read a *Playboy*!

ELDER MCKINLEY
We've ALL had the spooky hell
dream, people! I have it NIGHTLY.
The issue NOW is what the heck
am I supposed to tell the mission
president?!

Elder Price enters, still with blood on his shirt. He stops and just stares as the other Elders stare at him covered in blood.

ELDER CHURCH
Elder Price, what happened to YOU?

Price looks down at his blood-covered shirt for a beat, then –

ELDER PRICE
Africa...is NOTHING like *The Lion King* – I think that movie took a LOT of artistic license.

ELDER CUNNINGHAM
He's upset because we just saw a guy get shot in the face.

ELDERS
Oooh. / Ewww. / That's not good. / Etc.

ELDER PRICE
I cannot continue my mission this way! There is absolutely NOTHING I can accomplish here!

ELDER MCKINLEY
Elder Price, you cannot lose your cool on me now, we're about to get evaluated by the MISSION PRESIDENT!

ELDER PRICE
(getting an idea)
The mission president! That's it! I have to go see the mission president and get transferred!

ELDER CUNNINGHAM
Buddy! BUDDY! I know today was rough. But remember – tomorrow is a LATTER DAY!

Price gets in Cunningham's face.

ELDER PRICE
"LATTER DAY" DOESN'T MEAN TOMORROW!!!!
(beat)
IT MEANS THE RECKONING! THE AFTERLIFE! "LATTER DAYS" WHERE ALL GOOD PEOPLE GO TO HEAVENLY FATHER AND GET EVERYTHING THEY'VE ALWAYS WANTED!!!! I'M OUTTA HERE!

Price starts to leave.

ELDER MCKINLEY
Hey! HEY! Are you forgetting rule number twenty-three?! You cannot leave the living quarters after 9 PM!!

ELDER PRICE
To heck with the rules, I'm not wasting the most important two years of my life!

Price storms out.

ELDER CUNNINGHAM
Hey, hold up, you forgot me!

Elder Cunningham starts to go after him.

ELDER MCKINLEY
Elder Cunningham, do you ALSO

want to break rule number twenty-three?!

ELDER CUNNINGHAM
Oh NO! What am I supposed to do? According to rule number twenty-three I can't leave the living quarters after curfew – but according to rule seventy-two I can never let my companion be alone! This is like a *Matrix* logic trick! Rule seventy-two – rule twenty-three – rule seventy-two – I'M SORRY GUYS! HE'S MY BEST FRIEND!

Cunningham slams the door, leaving.

- THE VILLAGE -

Price is at the bus station where he and Cunningham first arrived. Cunningham comes chasing after him.

ELDER CUNNINGHAM
ELDER PRICE! ELDER PRICE WAIT UP!! HEY COME ON!! We gotta be together at all times, remember?!

ELDER PRICE
I can't do something incredible here!

Elder Price starts walking away but Cunningham spins him around and grabs his shoulders.

ELDER CUNNINGHAM
OKAY, STOP! Breathe. THINK. This isn't what you want to do.

ELDER PRICE
Yes it IS.

ELDER CUNNINGHAM
Alright, if you want to transfer... then THAT'S WHAT WE'RE DOING!! I'm with you, buddy!!!

ELDER PRICE
I didn't say WE'RE transferring – I said I AM.

Elder Cunningham looks like he's been slapped.

ELDER CUNNINGHAM
(hurt)
Oh... I see...

ELDER PRICE
(sighs, then –)
Look, I'm sorry, but you and I just aren't that compatible, alright?

ELDER CUNNINGHAM
Well, we only became best friends a few days ago! Maybe I could –

ELDER PRICE
I'M NOT YOUR BEST FRIEND! I was just STUCK with you by the missionary training center.

Now Cunningham looks really hurt.

ELDER PRICE
I didn't MEAN to say "STUCK"... It's just that.

ELDER CUNNINGHAM
Yeah, yeah no it's cool. I know how it goes. It's really fine. I'll be totally fine...

ELDER PRICE
You WILL be fine, we just need, you know, different things.

ELDER CUNNINGHAM
Right, different things.

ELDER PRICE
(sighs and then slowly offers –)
It was...nice meeting you.

ELDER CUNNINGHAM
(trying not to cry)
Yeah. Yeah, awesome. Take it easy.

Price walks away. Cunningham takes a few steps in different directions, not really sure what to do or where to go.

I AM HERE FOR YOU (REPRISE)

ELDER CUNNINGHAM
EVENING STAR SHINES BRIGHTLY
GOD MAKES LIFE ANEW.
TOMORROW IS A LATTER DAY
I WAS THERE FOR YOU.

*Leave Cunningham alone and quiet for a while, really let this moment land. Silence...
Finally, Nabulungi enters –*

NABULUNGI
There you are!

She rushes toward Cunningham.

NABULUNGI
Thank goodness I found you! Where is your friend?

ELDER CUNNINGHAM
I don't have any friends.

NABULUNGI
No, no! I have written Elder Price a text. Here!

She hands him a piece of paper.

NABULUNGI
It says to please come back to the village. We are ready!

ELDER CUNNINGHAM
To do what?

NABULUNGI
To LISTEN to him! I texted everyone we HAVE to give Elder Price a chance!

ELDER CUNNINGHAM
I'm sorry, he's transferring.

NABULUNGI
What is transferring?!

ELDER CUNNINGHAM
That means he'll be sent somewhere else.

NABULUNGI
No! He can't leave! We're ready to listen!

ELDER CUNNINGHAM
It's too late he's made up his mind.

She stares off in Price's direction, then turns back and sizes up Cunningham.

NABULUNGI
What about you?

ELDER CUNNINGHAM
Me? What?

NABULUNGI
He's gone. But you are still here. YOU can lead us. Teach us everything about what's in the Book of Mormon.

ELDER CUNNINGHAM
Me? No, no... I'm a FOLLOWER.

NABULUNGI
Everyone is waiting! Just come back to the village and YOU WILL HAVE YOUR LISTENERS! I SWEAR IT!!!!

She dashes away, leaving Cunningham alone to think.

Finally, he breaks out into song.

MAN UP

ELDER CUNNINGHAM
WHAT DID JESUS DO,
    WHEN THEY SENTENCED HIM TO
    DIE?
DID HE TRY TO RUN AWAY?
DID HE JUST BREAK DOWN AND
    CRY?

NO, JESUS DUG DOWN DEEP,
    KNOWING WHAT HE HAD TO DO
WHEN FACED WITH HIS OWN
    DEATH,
JESUS KNEW THAT HE HAD TO...

MAN UP.
HE HAD TO MAN UP.
SO HE CRAWLED UP ON THAT
    CROSS,
AND HE STUCK IT OUT.
HE MANNED UP.
CHRIST, HE MANNED UP.
AND TAUGHT US ALL WHAT REAL
    MANNING UP IS ABOUT.

AND NOW IT'S UP TO ME

AND IT'S TIME TO MAN UP.
JESUS HAD HIS TIME TA,
NOW ITS MINE TA MAN UP.
I'M TAKING THE REINS,
I'M CROSSING THE BEAR –
AND JUST LIKE JESUS,
I'M GROWING A PAIR!
I'VE GOTTA STAND UP,
CAN'T JUST CLAM UP,
ITS TIME TA MAN UP!

(Dance Break)

CUZ THERE'S A TIME IN YOUR LIFE
    WHEN YOU KNOW YOU'VE GOT
    TO MAN UP!
DON'T LET IT PASS YOU BY
THERE'S JUST ONE TIME TA MAN
    UP!
WATCH ME MAN UP LIKE NOBODY
    ELSE!
I'M GONNA MAN UP ALL OVER
    MYSELF!
I'VE GOT TO GET READY,
IT'S TIME TA
TIME TA.

WHAT DID JESUS DO
    WHEN THEY PUT NAILS THROUGH
    HIS HANDS?
DID HE SCREAM LIKE A GIRL OR
    DID HE TAKE IT LIKE A MAN?
WHEN SOMEONE HAD TO DIE
    TO SAVE US FROM OUR SINS
JESUS SAID "I'LL DO IT" AND HE
    TOOK IT ON THE CHIN!
HE MANNED UP!
HE MANNED UP.
HE TOOK A BULLET FOR ME AND
    YOU,
THAT'S MAN UP.
REAL MAN UP.
AND NOW IT'S MY TIME TAAAA –

AND NOW IT'
AND IT'S
MA
JESUS HAD
NOW IT'
MA

S UP TO ME

TIME TO

UP.

IS TIME TA,

MINE TA

UP.

DO IT, TOO.
TIME TO BE A HERO AND SLAY
THE MONSTER!
TIME TO BATTLE DARKNESS –
YOU'RE NOT MY FAT-HER!
I'M GONNA TIME TA, JUST WATCH
ME GO!
IT'S TIME TA STEP UP AND STEAL
THE SHOW!
IT'S TIME TA! IT'S MINE TA! IT'S
TIME TA!
TIME TA TIME TA –

*Nabulungi, on another part of
the stage, singing to some of the
Ugandans.*

NABULUNGI
SAL TLAY KA SITI -
A PLACE OF HOPE AND JOY

ELDER CUNNINGHAM
MAN UP!

NABULUNGI
AND IF WE WANT TO GO THERE
WE JUST HAVE TO FOLLOW THAT
WHITE BOY

ELDER CUNNINGHAM
TIME TA!

*Now reveal Elder Price. He looks
like he's painfully hot and in need of
water as he wanders around, lost.*

ELDER PRICE
HEAVENLY FATHER WHY DO YOU
LET BAD THINGS HAPPEN?

UGANDANS
KA-LAY-KA CITY!

NABULUNGI
DID YOU GET MY TEXT?

ELDER PRICE
MORE TO THE POINT WHY DO YOU
LET BAD THINGS HAPPEN TO ME?

UGANDANS
KA-LAY-KAA
WE GOT YOUR TEXT!

ELDER PRICE
I'M SURE YOU DON'T THINK I'M A
FLAKE

ELDER CUNNINGHAM
MAN UP!

ELDER PRICE
BECAUSE YOU'VE CLEARLY MADE A
MISTAKE.

ELDERS
TURN IT OFF!

ELDER PRICE
I'M GOING WHERE YOU NEED ME
MOST –
ORLANDO!!!

CHORUS
ORLANDO!

UGANDANS
WE WILL LISTEN TO THAT FAT
WHITE GUY!

ELDER CUNNINGHAM
MY TIME TO TIME TA
NOW IT'S MY TIME TO TIME TA!

UGANDANS
BUT HASA DIGA EEBOWAI!

ELDER CUNNINGHAM
NO TIME TA, NOT TIME TA,
NO NOW IT'S TIME TO TIME TA!

UGANDANS
HUUH!

ELDER CUNNINGHAM
I'M IN THE LEAD FOR THE
VERY FIRST TIME!

UGANDANS
TIME TA

ELDER PRICE
I'M GOING WHERE THE SUN
ALWAYS SHINES

UGANDANS
SHINES TA
HAAAA

ELDER CUNNINGHAM
I'VE GOT TO STAND UP
GET MY FLIPPIN' CAN UP

NABULUNGI
SAL TLAY KA SITI –
SAL TLAY KA SITI –
SAL TLAY KA SITI –

UGANDANS
HAY YA YA
HAY YA YA
HAY YA YA HA

ELDER PRICE
ORLANDO!
ORLANDO!
I'M COMING
ORLANDO!

ELDER CUNNINGHAM
IT IS TIME TA –!

GOTSWANA
I HAVE MAGGOTS IN MY SCROTUM!

ACT 2

THE BOOK OF MORMON

-PROLOGUE-
THE HILL OF CUMORAH

The pageant starts once again, with the same fanfare as before. Joseph Smith is kneeling, holding the golden plates as if he has just dug them up. Near him, a scene of Christ appearing to the ancient Americans.

NARRATOR
And yea, it came to pass that the Prophet Joseph Smith discovered the Book of Mormon on golden plates. But what exactly is the Book of Mormon ABOUT? It tells of two Hebrew tribes at war in ancient America – the gentle Nephites, and the wicked Lamanites. They fought many great battles, but then, just after his crucifixion, Christ appeared!

Christ appears, as before.

JESUS
I am Jesus. I've just been crucified on the other side of the world, you guys. I only have three days before I am resurrected, but in that time, I will preach here to you in America.

NARRATOR
And LO, Christ told them many things, and a Nephite named

Mormon wrote the teachings on golden plates. Plates that became the Book of Mormon! A book that is still today read by missionaries all over the world!!!

- THE VILLAGE -

Cunningham is with the Ugandans, reading from the Book of Mormon. Cunningham is trying to be a preacher, but he really doesn't have what it takes.

ELDER CUNNINGHAM
(reading with vigor)
And it came to pass that the... that the NEPHITES had gathered together a great number of men, even to exceed the number of thirty thousand! And it came to pass that they did have in this same year a number of battles, in which the Nephites did beat the Lamanites and did slay many of them!

Cunningham seems to finish – the Ugandans just stare at him.

UGANDAN WOMAN
So what the fuck does THAT mean?

Cunningham obviously has no idea as he scratches his head...

ELDER CUNNINGHAM
Uh... That MEANS... You know... You should... Be NICE to each other or something.
(clears throat then goes on reading –)
And lo, God was so displeased with the Lamanites that he caused a cursing to come upon them. Wherefore as they WERE WHITE and delightsome, the Lord God

did cause a skin of BLACKNESS to come upon them! And thus oooh – ughhh...

Cunningham sees that the Ugandans look insulted.

ELDER CUNNINGHAM
Uh, sorry, hang on, let's skip to another part...

Cunningham turns and flips through the pages.

MAFALA
(to Nabulungi)
How is THIS supposed to make things better for us? General Butt-Fucking Naked is going to come back and if he sees us here we are all DEAD.

NABULUNGI
Baba, please, we just need to LISTEN.

MIDDALA
To WHAT?!
(standing up)
THREE HOURS we been listening to him talk about STUPID SHIT that happened on the other side of the Earth thousands of years ago! It has nothing to do with US!

SADAKA
That's right! Those "NEPHITES" probably didn't even have AIDS to deal with!

UGANDANS
(angry, leaving)
Yeah! / That's right! / Shit! / Etc.

ELDER CUNNINGHAM
UH SURE THEY DID! SURE THEY DID!! People back then had even

WORSE AIDS!

Everyone quiets down and listens to him.

ELDER CUNNINGHAM
Yeah!

Cunningham pretends to look through the Book of Mormon, and then pretends to read from it –

ELDER CUNNINGHAM
(reading)
And LO! The Lord said unto the Nephites – I know you're really depressed, with all your AIDS and everything...But there is an answer in Christ!

The Ugandans look surprised. They are now paying attention to Cunningham.

NABULUNGI
You see?! This book CAN help us!

As everyone turns and chatters to Nabulungi, Cunningham goes to his own corner of the stage.

MAKING THINGS UP AGAIN

ELDER CUNNINGHAM
I JUST TOLD A LIE.
Wait, no I didn't lie...
I JUST USED MY IMAGINATION.
And it worked!

Cunningham's dad appears in Cunningham's imagination.

CUNNINGHAM'S DAD
YOU'RE MAKING THINGS UP AGAIN,
ARNOLD.

ELDER CUNNINGHAM
Yeah, but it worked, dad!

CUNNINGHAM'S DAD
YOU'RE STRETCHING THE TRUTH
AGAIN,
AND YOU KNOW IT

Joseph Smith appears on another side of the stage.

JOSEPH SMITH
DON'T BE A FIBBING FRAN,
ARNOLD

ELDER CUNNINGHAM
Joseph Smith?

JOSEPH SMITH & DAD
BECAUSE A LIE IS A LIE.

ELDER CUNNINGHAM
It's not a lie!

Now Mormon and Moroni from the previous pageant come back to life.

CHORUS
YOU'RE MAKING THINGS UP AGAIN,
ARNOLD!

ELDER CUNNINGHAM
Oh, conscience.

CHORUS
YOU'RE TAKING THE HOLY WORD
AND ADDING FICTION!
BE CAREFUL HOW YOU PROCEED,
ARNOLD.
WHEN YOU FIB, THERE'S A PRICE.

MUTUMBO
This is bullshit! The story I'VE been told is that the way to cure AIDS is by sleeping with a virgin! I'm gonna go and rape a baby!

ELDER CUNNINGHAM
WHAT!?!! OH MY – NO! You can't do that!
(scolding like a dog–)
NO!!!!

MUTUMBO
Why not?

ELDER CUNNINGHAM
Because that is DEFINITELY against God's way!

MUTUMBO
Says who!? Where in that book of yours does it say ANYTHING about having sex with a baby?! Nowhere!

Cunningham looks through his book confused.

MUTUMBO
Nowhere!

Mutumbo starts to leave.

ELDER CUNNINGHAM
Uhhh, behold –

YOU'RE THINK AGA ARN

MAKING

GS UP

AIN,

OLD.

(*pretending to read*)
The Lord said to the Mormon
Joseph Smith, "You shall not have
sex with that infant!"

*Everyone stops and turns to
Cunningham.*

ELDER CUNNINGHAM
(*pretending to read more,
stammering*)
LO! Joseph said, "Why not, Lord?"
And thusly the Lord said, "If you lay
with an infant you shall burn in the
fiery pits of Mordor."

MUTUMBO
Really?

ELDER CUNNINGHAM
"A baby cannot cure your illness,
Joseph Smith – I shall give unto
you... A FROG..." And thus Joseph
laid with the frog and his AIDS was
no more!

UGANDANS
Ohhhhhh....

CHORUS
YOU'RE MAKING THINGS UP AGAIN,
ARNOLD.
YOU'RE RECKLESSLY WARPING THE
WORDS OF JESUS!

*Now a light comes on two
hobbit-like creatures, holding
swords and on their knees with
big fake hairy feet.*

HOBBITS
YOU CAN'T JUST SAY WHAT YOU
WANT, ARNOLD.

ELDER CUNNINGHAM
Come on, hobbits.

HOBBITS & CHORUS
YOU'RE DIGGING YOURSELF A DEEP
HOLE.

ELDER CUNNINGHAM
I'M MAKING THINGS UP AGAIN,
KIND OF!
BUT THIS TIME IT'S HELPING A
DOZEN PEOPLE!
THERE'S NOTHING SO BAD
BECAUSE THIS TIME –
I'M NOT COMMITTING A SIN
JUST BY MAKING THINGS UP AGAIN,
RIGHT?!

CHORUS
NO!

NABULUNGI
Elder Cunningham! You have to
stop him!

ELDER CUNNINGHAM
What? What is it?

NABULUNGI
Gotswana is going to cut off his
daughter's clitoris!

ELDER CUNNINGHAM
HAH?!

GOTSWANA
This is all very interesting, but
women HAVE to be circumcised if
it's what The General wants!

ELDER CUNNINGHAM
No, no, doing that to a lady is
against Christ's will!

GOTSWANA
How do you know? Christ never
said nothin' about no clitoris!

{ 58 }

ELDER CUNNINGHAM
Yes! Yes he did!
(pretending to read)
In ancient New York, three men
were about to cut off a Mormon
woman's clitoris! But right before
they did – Jesus had Boba Fett turn
them into FROGS!

GOTSWANA
Frogs?

UGANDAN WOMAN
You mean like the frogs that got
fucked by Joseph Smith!

ELDER CUNNINGHAM
Yeah! Those frogs! "For a clitoris is
holy amongst all things," said he!

CHORUS
YOU'RE MAKING THINGS UP AGAIN,
ARNOLD.

UGANDANS
WE'RE LEARNING THE TRUTH!

CHORUS
YOU'RE TAKING THE HOLY WORD
AND ADDING FICTION!

UGANDANS
THE TRUTH ABOUT GOD.

CHORUS
BE CAREFUL HOW YOU PROCEED,
ARNOLD.
WHEN YOU FIB THERE'S A PRICE.

UGANDAN
WE'RE GOING TO PARADISE.

ELDER CUNNINGHAM
Right!

ELDER CUNNINGHAM
WHO WOULD HAVE THOUGHT I

HAD THIS MAGIC TOUCH?
WHO'D HAVE BELIEVED I COULD
MAN UP THIS MUCH?
I'M TALKING, THEY'RE LISTENING,
MY STORIES ARE GLISTENING
I'M GONNA SAVE THEM
ALL WITH THIS STUFF!

UGANDANS
OOHH - LA

CHORUS
YOU'RE MAKING THINGS UP
AGAIN, ARNOLD!

UGANDANS
ELDER CUNNINGHAM!

CHORUS
YOU'RE MAKING THINGS UP
AGAIN, ARNOLD!

UGANDANS
HOLY PROPHET MAN!

CHORUS
YOU'RE MAKING THINGS UP
AGAIN, ARNOLD.

UGANDANS
Our savior!

ELDER CUNNINGHAM
YOU'RE MAKING THINGS UP
AGAIN...

YODA
Up again making things you are –

ELDER CUNNINGHAM
ARNOLD...

- THE DREAM -

The curtain opens to find Elder

{ 59 }

*Price with his backpack happily
bouncing through Orlando.
Very happy Disney-style MUSIC
plays as Price bops around like a
tourist, scoping things out.*

ELDER PRICE
I'm here!! I'm here!

*He drops his bag and spins
around like Mary Tyler Moore.*

ELDER PRICE
I'MMMM HEEEERE!!!

*Price walks up to the audience
and explains–*

EDLER PRICE
Orlando! And it's even BETTER
than I could have imagined! The
streets are clean, the people are
happy...

Something catches his eye.

ELDER PRICE
Epcot Center! I can see the ball!

*But then a quizzical look comes
over him.*

ELDER PRICE
The funny thing is... I don't really
remember getting here...

*Price now seems a little
confused as the music changes to
something slightly dreamy.*

ELDER PRICE
Wait... This can't be Orlando... I
don't even remember the plane
landing.

Things start to get dark –

ELDER PRICE
What's happened to me? Where am I?

*A CLAP OF THUNDER THEN
A BOOMING VOICE FROM
OFFSTAGE –*

SATAN
Kevin Price!

ELDER PRICE
Who is that?!

SATAN
You broke the rules, Elder... Your
soul belongs to ME now!

ELDER PRICE
... Mickey?

SATAN
Ha Ha HA! Think again, minion!
You now dwell in eternal flame.

A CRASH OF THUNDER.

ELDER PRICE
Oh no! I remember this place...

*The lights go red as Price starts
to figure it out.*

**SPOOKY MORMON
HELL DREAM**

ELDER PRICE
 LONG AGO WHEN I WAS FIVE
 I SNUCK IN THE KITCHEN LATE AT
  NIGHT
 AND ATE A DONUT WITH A MAPLE
  GLAZE.

Some EERIE sounds.

ELDER PRICE

MY FATHER ASKED WHO ATE THE
   SNACK
I SAID THAT IT WAS MY BROTHER
   JACK
AND JACK GOT GROUNDED FOR
   FOURTEEN DAYS.

More EERIE sounds.

ELDER PRICE

I'VE LIVED WITH THE GUILT ALL OF
   MY LIFE.
AND THE TERRIBLE VISION THAT I
   HAD THAT NIGHT

*Price takes a falling pose and
screams –*

ELDER PRICE

NO PLEASE! I DON'T WANNA GO
   BAAAAAAACK!!!!!

*Now the stage is fully revealed
as Price lands in Hell. The cast,
dressed in various demonic
outfits, crowds in around him.*

CHORUS

DOWN, DOWN THY SOUL IS
   CAST!
FROM THE EARTH WHENCE FORTH
   YE FELL!
THE PATH OF FIRE LEADS THEE –
TO SPOOKY MORMON HELL
   DREAM!
WELCOME BACK TO
   SPOOKY MORMON HELL DREAM!
YOU ARE HAVING
   A SPOOKY MORMON HELL
   DREAM NOW!

ELDER PRICE

AND NOW I'VE GONE AND DONE IT
   AGAIN

CHORUS

RECTUS!

ELDER PRICE

I'VE COMMITTED ANOTHER
   AWFUL SIN

CHORUS

DOMINUS!

ELDER PRICE

I LEFT MY MISSION COMPANION
   ALL ALONE.

CHORUS

SPOOKYTUS!

ELDER PRICE

OH GOD, HOW COULD I HAVE
   DONE THIS TO YOU?

CHORUS

DEUS!

ELDER PRICE

HOW COULD I BREAK
   RULE SEVENTY-TWO?

CHORUS

CREEPYUS!

{ 61 }

AND NOW MY SOUL HA

BACK

SPO

MOR

HELL

H JUST BEEN THROWN

INTO

OKY MON

REAM!

ELDER PRICE

> AND NOW MY SOUL HATH JUST
>> BEEN THROWN
> BACK INTO SPOOKY MORMON
>> HELL DREAM!

CHORUS

> DOWN DOWN TO SATAN'S REALM,
> SEE WHERE YOU BELONG!
> THERE IS NOTHING YOU CAN DO,
> NO ESCAPE FROM SPOOKY
>> MORMON HELL DREAM!

JESUS appears.

JESUS

You blamed your brother for eating the donut and now you walk out on your mission companion?! You're a DICK!

ELDER PRICE

Jesus, I'm sorry!

Price chases after Jesus but is stopped by Hell's residents.

CHORUS

> JESUS HATES YOU THIS WE KNOW!
> FOR JESUS JUST TOLD YOU SO!

SKELETON 1

> YOU REMEMBER LUCIFER!

SKELETON 2

> HE IS EVEN SPOO-KI-ER!

Satan appears.

SATAN

> MINIONS OF HADES, HAVE YOU
>> HEARD THE NEWS?
> KEVIN WAS CAUGHT PLAYING
>> HOOKY!
> NOW HE'S BACK WITH ALL YOU
>> CATH'LICS AND JEWS.
> IT'S SUPER SPOOKY WOOKY.

ELDER PRICE

> I'M SORRY LORD IT WAS SELFISH OF ME
>> TO BREAK THE RULES,
> PLEASE I DON'T WANNA BE
>> IN THIS SPOOKY MORMON HELL
>> DREAM!

CHORUS

> SPOOKY MORMON HELL DREAM!
> GENGHIS KHAN,
> JEFFREY DAHMER,
> HITLER,
> JOHNNY COCHRAN!
> THEIR SPIRITS ALL SURROUND
>> YOU!
> SPOOKY SPOOKY SPOOOOKY!

ADOLPH HITLER

> I STARTED A WAR AND KILLED
>> MILLIONS OF JEWS!

GENGHIS KHAN

> I SLAUGHTERED THE CHINESE!

JEFFERY DAHMER

> I STABBED A GUY AND FUCKED HIS
>> CORPSE!

JOHNNY COCHRAN

I GOT OJ FREED!

ELDER PRICE

YOU THINK THAT'S BAD? I BROKE
RULE SEVENTY-TWO!

**HITLER / KHAN / DAHMER /
COCHRAN**

HOH?!?!

ELDER PRICE

I LEFT MY COMPANION!
I'M WAY WORSE THAN YOU!
(shouting)
I HATE THIS SPOOKY MORMON
HELL DREAM!

CHORUS

SPOOKY MORMON HELL DREAM!

ELDER PRICE

(looking up, praying)
Please, Heavenly Father! Give me
one more chance! I won't break the
rules again!

*Members of Hell dance around
Price, taunting him. Two
dancing coffee cups enter.*

ELDER PRICE

No more, please no more!

CHORUS

SPOOKY MORMON HELL DREAM!
SPOOKY MORMON HELL DREAM!

Demons make Price drink coffee.

CHORUS

Chug! Chug! Chug! Chug!

ELDER PRICE

Dad, dad! I'm so glad you're here!

Price dances with demons.

ELDER PRICE

I CAN'T BELIEVE JESUS CALLED ME
A DICK!!!!

CHORUS

WELCOME, WELCOME
TO SPOOKY MORMON HELL
DREAM!
YOU ARE NEVER WAKING UP FROM
SPOOKY MORMON HELL DREAM!
DOWN DOWN, THY SOUL IS CAST
FROM THE EARTH WHENCE FORTH
YE FELL.
THIS MUST BE IT YOU MUST BE
THERE, YOU MUST BE IN
SPOOKY MORMON HELL DREAM
NOW!

ELDER PRICE

No! Please let me wake up, I'll do
anything!!! Please, Heavenly Father,
I won't let you down again!

CHORUS

SPOOKY MORMON HELL DREAM
DONE!

- THE VILLAGE -

*After the pounding applause,
Elder Price finds himself lying*

on the ground surrounded by the other missionaries.

ELDER MCKINLEY
I think he's coming to! Come on, Elder Price... Wake up, buddy...

ELDER PRICE
Wha– What? Where am I?

ELDER DAVIS
Looks like you fell asleep at the bus station!

ELDER CHURCH
We were SO worried!

ELDER PRICE
I'm sorry, OK?! I'm sorry I had a little meltdown last night. I'm not leaving, alright? I...realized while I was asleep that it's WRONG and I've got to stick to my work.

ELDER MCKINLEY
Ohh, you had the Hell Dream, didn't you...

Humming, Elder Cunningham enters.

ELDER CUNNINGHAM
OH, HEY GUYS!

ELDER MICHAELS
Elder Cunningham! Where have YOU been?!

ELDER CUNNINGHAM
Oh, nowhere much...
(proud of himself)
Just with TEN EAGER AFRICANS who are now interested in the church!

The Elders all rush around Cunningham.

ELDERS
WHAT?! / Are you serious?! / Oh my God?! / Etc.

ELDER CUNNINGHAM
Yup... Yup they're all completely into the teachings and willing to learn more!

Now Price rushes up to Cunningham.

ELDER PRICE
Are you serious, Elder Cunningham?! That's amazing!

ELDER CUNNINGHAM
(hurt girlfriend)
Oh. Elder Price. Hey.

ELDER PRICE
Hey...

ELDER CUNNINGHAM
So, did you find yourself a new companion?

ELDER PRICE
No. No, I'm sorry about that... But this is GREAT, Elder Cunningham! If you've got some eager followers we can really turn things around. I think we should start preparing which verses to teach them and then we can prep some exercises –

ELDER CUNNINGHAM
Uh woa – woa. You LEFT me. Remember?

ELDER DAVIS
Elder Cunningham we must always work in PAIRS. Remember?

ELDER MCKINLEY
Give Elder Cunningham a break – if it's working better this way, he can

leave Elder Price out of it.

ELDERS
Yeah! / Right! / I agree! / Etc.

The Elders all crowd around Cunningham – almost pushing Price out of the way.

ELDER MCKINLEY
Now, how many of the people want to have follow-up sessions?!

ELDER CUNNINGHAM
Oh, let's see... All of them!

ELDERS
All of them! / Oh my gosh! / Wow! / You're amazing, Elder Cunningham!

Price walks off to a private section of the stage.

ELDER CHURCH
Do you think we might actually get a baptism out of this?

ELDER MCKINLEY
They always say if you can just get that FIRST BAPTISM others will follow!

ELDER CUNNINGHAM
Hold on, guys... I know I'm doing a real good job and all, but... Let's not get too carried away. I mean... A lot of these people are scared to death of that "General Butt-F-ing Naked" guy.

ELDERS
(a bit deflated)
Oh, yeah. / Oh, that guy... / The General... / Etc.

ELDER THOMAS
Well, somebody needs to tell that

General Butt-F-ing Naked that people should be free to do what they want!

ELDER MCKINLEY
Nobody is going to change how a crazy warlord thinks! That would take something INCREDIBLE.

A DING goes off. A light shines on Price's face.

ELDER PRICE
(realizing)
> SOMETHING... INCREDIBLE...
> SOMETHING INCREDIBLE...

ELDER MCKINLEY
(ignoring Price)
Well, look, let's just be happy that Elder Cunningham has people interested.

ELDERS
That's true! / Yeah! / At least we have that! / Etc.

Price suddenly bursts in front of them – filled with new energy.

ELDER PRICE
It's alright, guys! I've got everything under control!! I know what the Lord wants from me now! This village is gonna be SAVED!

ELDERS
So anyways... / Great! / Come on... / Etc.

The Elders walk off, leaving Price on stage alone and confused.

I BELIEVE

ELDER PRICE

EVER SINCE I WAS A CHILD
I TRIED TO BE THE BEST...
SO WHAT HAPPENED?
MY FAMILY AND FRIENDS ALL SAID I
WAS BLESSED....
SO WHAT HAPPENED?

The song picks up.

ELDER PRICE

IT WAS SUPPOSED TO BE ALL SO
EXCITING
TO BE TEACHING OF CHRIST 'CROSS
THE SEA.
BUT I ALLOWED MY FAITH TO BE
SHAKEN –
OH WHAT'S THE MATTER WITH ME?

I'VE ALWAYS LONGED TO HELP
THE NEEDY.
TO DO THE THINGS I'VE NEVER
DARED.
THIS WAS THE TIME FOR ME
TO STEP UP.
SO THEN WHY WAS I SO SCARED?

A WARLORD THAT SHOOTS PEOPLE
IN THE FACE.
WHAT'S SO SCARY ABOUT THAT?
I MUST TRUST THAT MY LORD
IS MIGHTIER –
AND ALWAYS HAS MY BACK.
NOW I MUST BE COMPLETELY
DEVOUT.
I CAN'T HAVE EVEN ONE SHRED
OF DOUBT!

I BELIEVE –
THAT THE LORD GOD CREATED
THE UNIVERSE.
I BELIEVE –
THAT HE SENT HIS ONLY SON TO DIE
FOR MY SINS.
AND I BELIEVE –
THAT ANCIENT JEWS BUILT BOATS
AND SAILED TO AMERICA.
I AM A MORMON, AND A MORMON
JUST BELIEVES.

YOU CANNOT JUST BELIEVE PART-
WAY.
YOU HAVE TO BELIEVE IN IT ALL.
MY PROBLEM WAS DOUBTING THE
LORD'S WILL,
INSTEAD OF STANDING TALL.
I CAN'T ALLOW MYSELF TO HAVE
ANY DOUBT.
IT'S TIME TO SET MY WORRIES FREE.
TIME TO SHOW THE WORLD WHAT
ELDER PRICE IS ABOUT
AND SHARE THE POWER INSIDE OF
ME!
I BELIEVE–

CHORUS

AHHH...

ELDER PRICE

THAT GOD HAS A PLAN FOR ALL OF
US.
I BELIEVE –

CHORUS

I BELIEVE AAHHH....

ELDER PRICE

THAT PLAN INVOLVES
ME GETTING MY OWN PLANET.
AND I BELIEVE

CHORUS

BELIEVE OHO...

ELDER PRICE

THAT THE CURRENT PRESIDENT OF
THE CHURCH, THOMAS MONSON,
SPEAKS DIRECTLY TO GOD.
I AM A MORMON AND, DANG IT,
A MORMON JUST BELIEVES.

CHORUS

A MORMON JUST BELIEVES.

ELDER PRICE

I KNOW THAT I MUST GO AND DO –
THE THINGS MY GOD COMMANDS.

CHORUS

THINGS MY GOD COMMANDS

ELDER PRICE

I REALIZE NOW WHY HE SENT ME
HERE!

CHORUS

AHHH! AHHH!

ELDER PRICE

IF YOU ASK THE LORD IN FAITH
HE WILL ALWAYS ANSWER YOU
JUST BELIEVE

CHORUS

JUST BELIEVE

ELDER PRICE

IN HIM AND HAVE NO FEAR!

- THE GENERAL'S CAMP -

*The General does what he can
to seem impressive. He sits on a
mound of guns and ammo.*

GENERAL'S GUARD
(entering)
General! We have an intruder! He
just walked right into camp!

Elder Price bursts into camp.

ELDER PRICE

I BELIEVE!!!!

CHORUS

AAHHH

ELDER PRICE

THAT SATAN HAS A HOLD OF YOU.

CHORUS

SATAN HAS A HOLD

*Everyone looks at each other,
confused.*

ELDER PRICE

I BELIEVE!

CHORUS

I BELIEVE!

ELDER PRICE

THAT THE LORD GOD HAS SENT ME
HERE!

CHORUS

GOD HAS SENT ME HERE

ELDER PRICE

AND I BELIEVE!

CHORUS

BELIEVE

ELDER PRICE

THAT IN 1978 GOD CHANGED HIS
MIND ABOUT BLACK PEOPLE!!!

CHORUS

BLACK PEOPLE!!!

ELDER PRICE & CHORUS

YOU'LL BE A MORMON!
A MORMON WHO JUST BELIEVES.

THE GENERAL
The fuck is this?

ELDER PRICE

AND NOW I CAN FEEL THE
EXCITEMENT.
THIS IS THE MOMENT I WAS BORN
TO DO.
AND I FEEL SO INCREDIBLE –
TO BE SHARING MY FAITH WITH
YOU.
THE SCRIPTURES SAY IF YOU ASK
IN FAITH,
IF YOU ASK GOD HIMSELF YOU'LL
KNOW.
BUT YOU MUST ASK HIM WITHOUT
ANY DOUBT,
AND LET YOUR SPIRIT GROW!

CHORUS

LET YOUR SPIRIT GROW!

*Price takes the General's hand
and pulls the confused warlord
up from his seat as if asking him
to join him in prayer.*

ELDER PRICE

I BELIEVE!

CHORUS

AAHHH

ELDER PRICE

THAT GOD LIVES ON A PLANET
CALLED KOLOB!
I BELIEVE!

CHORUS

I BELIEVE

ELDER PRICE

THAT JESUS HAS

ELDER PRICE & CHORUS

HIS OWN PLANET AS WELL.

CHORUS

BELIEVE...

ELDER PRICE

AND I BELIEVE
THAT THE GARDEN OF EDEN WAS
IN JACKSON COUNTY, MISSOURI.

CHORUS

OOOO....

ELDER PRICE

IF YOU BELIEVE, THE LORD WILL
REVEAL IT.
AND YOU'LL KNOW IT'S ALL TRUE –
YOU'LL JUST FEEL IT.
YOU'LL BE A MORMON!!!!
AND BY GOSH –

ELDER PRICE & CHORUS

A MORMON JUST BELIEVESSSSSS!!!!

ELDER PRICE

OH, I BELIEVE!

CHORUS

A MORMON JUST...

ELDER PRICE

I BELIEVE!

CHORUS
BELIEVES!

*After the applause, POW!! The
General hits the book out of
Price's hand.*

THE GENERAL
JUMAMOSI!!!

*The guards pounce on Price.
Price looks very scared.*

ELDER PRICE
NO! WAIT! God has spoken to me,
sir!

*The guards advance on Price
and slap him around.*

ELDER PRICE
BY THE POWER OF GOD
ALMIGHTY TOUCH ME NOT!!!
The power of Christ compels you!!!!

*Price contorts his body almost as
if he expects lightning to come
shooting out his hands –*

ELDER PRICE
NO! NO WAIT PLEASE!!! WHAT
ARE YOU – NO!!!!!

Very serious Les Misérables
*"Look Down"-style music starts
to play as the scene gets even
more violent. The Gereral begins
to remove his clothes. Price
screams at the top of his lungs
as he appears to be very close to
being killed.*

ELDER PRICE
AHGHGHHGHG
HGHGHGHGGH!!!!!

The curtain closes.

- THE VILLAGE -

*Cunningham is preaching and
pretending to read from the
Book of Mormon.*

ELDER CUNNINGHAM
And so, yeah, so then Christ said
to the Nephites, "be strong!" You
know?! "Just because Lamanites got
big Death Star weapons and stuff
doesn't mean they should run your
lives! There's more of you than there
are of them, you know? You should
always... stand up for yourselves,"
Christ said!

MIDDALA
Just like the way the Hobbits all
stood up to Brigham Young's killers!

ELDER CUNNINGHAM
Yes! Very good, Middala! So the
Nephites fought off the wicked
Lamanites and for punishment the
Lord God turned the Lamanites
YELLOW!

KALIMBA
Ooh! Like the Chinese!

ELDER CUNNINGHAM
Right! Right! Okay, we better stop
there for today. Hopefully we'll see
everyone tomorrow?

UGANDANS
Okay! / Bye! / Thank you!

UGANDAN WOMAN
*(to another Ugandan
while walking out)*
The Book is right. We must not fight
amongst each other! The Chinese
are the real problem!

MAFALA
I LOVE all these Mormon stories!
They are so fucking weird.

SADAKA
Elder Cunningham... I just want to
say thank Heavenly Father you are
here.

*Mafala and the Ugandans leave,
but Nabulungi stays with
Cunningham.*

NABULUNGI
I've never seen the people here
so happy. Even Baba... You are
amazing.

ELDER CUNNINGHAM
Aw, I really haven't done that
much...

NABULUNGI
But you have. I texted my friend
the story you told us about Joseph
Smith's battle with diarrhea. He said
all the people in his village read it!
You are a great man.

ELDER CUNNINGHAM
(overwhelmed)
I... I kind of AM, huh?

NABULUNGI
Do you think we're good enough
to join the Mormons? We are all
trying very hard! We are ready to do
whatever tasks you require of us!

ELDER CUNNINGHAM
You don't understand, there's
nothing they have to DO to become
a Mormon. We let anybody who
wants to join up! As long as they're
willing to commit to the church,
then we can baptize them!

NABULUNGI
Well then – would you like to...
Baptize me?

ELDER CUNNINGHAM
Sure, of course! That would be great!

NABULUNGI
Okay, let's do it!

*Cunningham immediately looks
nervous.*

ELDER CUNNINGHAM
Wha– you mean right now?

NABULUNGI
Why not?

ELDER CUNNINGHAM
Well, I...

*Cunningham walks away
nervously and rubs his palms.*

ELDER CUNNINGHAM
To be honest I've...never done it
before.

NABULUNGI
That's okay – neither have I.

*She smiles at him. He starts to
get really nervous.*

ELDER CUNNINGHAM
Oh yeah! Guess that's true!

She crosses back over to him.

NABULUNGI
Do you know HOW to baptize
someone new into the church?

ELDER CUNNINGHAM
Of course! It's something we study
over and over at the –

(forgetting what it's called–)
– Missionary Control Center.

NABULUNGI
Then please, Elder Cunningham,
I want to be baptized. I swear to
dedicate my life to the church.

ELDER CUNNINGHAM
Ha... Okay, uh, I'm gonna need a
little time to get ready.

NABULUNGI
Okay, I'll get ready, too.

*They go to opposite ends of the
stage. Cunningham sets his Book of
Mormon down and starts to wash his
hands. Nabulungi pulls her hair back
to get ready to get wet.*

BAPTIZE ME

ELDER CUNNINGHAM
I'M ABOUT TO DO IT FOR THE
    FIRST TIME
AND I'M GONNA DO IT WITH A
    GIRL!
A SPECIAL GIRL –
WHO MAKES MY HEART KIND OF
    FLUTTER
MAKES MY EYES KIND OF BLUR –
I CAN'T BELIEVE I'M ABOUT TO
    BAPTIZE HER!

NABULUNGI
HE WILL BAPTIZE ME!
HE'LL HOLD ME IN HIS ARMS
AND HE WILL BAPTIZE ME.
RIGHT IN FRONT OF EVERYONE
AND IT WILL SET ME FREE –
WHEN HE LOOKS INTO MY EYES –
AND HE SEES JUST HOW MUCH
I LOVE BEING BAPTIZED...

ELDER CUNNINGHAM
I'M GONNA BAPTIZE HER.

NABULUNGI
BAPTIZE ME

ELDER CUNNINGHAM
BATHE HER IN GOD'S GLORY
AND I WILL BAPTIZE HER

NABULUNGI
I'M READY

ELDER CUNNINGHAM
WITH EVERYTHING I GOT.
AND I'LL MAKE HER BEG FOR
    MORE,

NABULUNGI
OOH

ELDER CUNNINGHAM

AS I WASH HER FREE FROM SIN.
AND IT'LL BE SO GOOD SHE'LL
WANT ME TO

**ELDER CUNNINGHAM &
NABULUNGI**

BAPTIZE HER/ME AGAIN.

*Finally they come together,
almost like they're going to kiss,
but then Cunningham suddenly
loses his nerve and backs away.*

ELDER CUNNINGHAM

Uh – I'm gonna need another
minute – excuse me.

*He walks away and Nabulungi
stares off at him.*

NABULUNGI

NEVER KNOWN A BOY SO GENTLE.
ONE LIKE HIM IS HARD TO FIND –
A SPECIAL KIND
IT MAKES MY HEART KIND OF
FLUTTER
LIKE A MOTH IN THE COCOON.
I HOPE HE GETS TO BAPTIZING ME
SOON.

*Cunningham comes back after
having collected himself.*

ELDER CUNNINGHAM

I'M GONNA BAPTIZE YOU.
I'M THROUGH WITH ALL MY
STALLING.

NABULUNGI

YOU'RE GONNA BAPTIZE ME.
I'M READY TO LET YOU DO IT.

BOTH

AND IT WILL SET US FREE.
IT'S TIME TO BE IMMERSED.
AND I'M SO HAPPY YOU'RE ABOUT
TO BE MY FIRST.

ELDER CUNNINGHAM

Okay, you ready?

NABULUNGI

I'm ready. So how do we do it?

ELDER CUNNINGHAM

Well, I hold you like this –

NABULUNGI

Yeah?

ELDER CUNNINGHAM

And I lower you down –

NABULUNGI
Yeah?

ELDER CUNNINGHAM
And then –

He drops her and she gets soaking wet. Suddenly Cunningham bursts out –

ELDER CUNNINGHAM
I JUST BAPTIZED HER!
SHE GOT DOUSED BY HEAVENLY
FATHER!
I JUST BAPTIZED HER GOOD!

NABULUNGI
YOU BAPTIZED ME!

ELDER CUNNINGHAM
I PERFORMED LIKE A CHAMP!

NABULUNGI
I'M WET WITH SALVATION!

BOTH
WE JUST WENT ALL THE WAY.
PRAISE BE TO GOD I'LL NEVER
FORGET THIS DAY...

ELDER CUNNINGHAM
I BAPTIZED YOU!

NABULUNGI
YOU BAPTIZED ME!

ELDER CUNNINGHAM
I GOTCHA GOOD!

NABULUNGI
BAPTIZE ME

ELDER CUNNINGHAM
YOU WANT IT MORE, BABY?

NABULUNGI
BAPTIZE ME!

The scene ends with the two looking at each other tenderly.

NABULUNGI
I'll text you later.

- DIRTY RIVER NEAR THE VILLAGE -

A new, more church-like and happy vamp of "Baptize Me" plays as we see all the Mormon Elders, except for Price and Cunningham, wearing white and getting ready to baptize the Ugandan people.

As the baptisms continue in the background, Elder McKinley steps forward into a light and dictates as if writing a letter.

ELDER MCKINLEY
Dear Mission President, it is my HONOR to inform you that the elders of Uganda District 9 have brought TWENTY NEW MEMBERS into the church...

Now a new person, the MISSION PRESIDENT, steps forward into a light reading the note.

MISSION PRESIDENT
...They are all fully committed to the Church of Jesus Christ of Latter-Day Saints, and our numbers continue to grow!
(no longer reading)
This is outstanding! These boys have converted more Africans than any district in the COUNTRY!

The mission president again steps forward this time as if reading from a letter HE wrote.

MISSION PRESIDENT
Elders of District 9! You have truly honored the church by your success! Congratulations on becoming ONE with the people of Africa!

McKinley steps forward.

I AM AFRICA

ELDER MCKINLEY
I AM AFRICA...
I AM AFRICA.
WITH THE STRENGTH OF
    THE CHEETAH,
MY NATIVE VOICE SHALL SING

ELDERS
WE ARE AFRICA!
WE ARE THE HEARTBEAT OF AF-RI-CA!

ELDER SCHRADER
WITH THE RHINO

ELDER THOMAS
THE MEERKAT

ELDER CHURCH
THE NOBLE LION KING

ELDERS
WE ARE AFRICA!
WE ARE THE WINDS OF THE
    SERENGETI,
WE ARE THE SWEAT OF THE
    JUNGLE MAN
WE ARE THE TEARS OF NELSON
    MANDELA –
WE ARE THE LOST BOYS OF
    THE SUDAN.

Now Cunningham steps out through the line of Elders, with Nabulungi.

ELDER CUNNINGHAM
I AM AFRICA!
JUST LIKE BONO! I AM AFRICA!
I FLEW IN HERE AND BECAME
    ONE WITH THIS LAND!

ELDERS

HA NA HEYA! AZ BA NEYBA!

ELDER CUNNINGHAM

I'M NOT A FOLLOWER ANYMORE
    NO! NOW, I AM FRICKIN' AFRICA!
WITH MY ZULU SPEAR, I RUN
    BAREFOOT THROUGH THE SAND!
I AM AFRICA!

ELDERS

AHH,
HA NA HEY A ZABA NEYBA.
HA NA HEY A ZABA NEY. AHH!
AH AH AH AH AII AIIA AH-T

*As the song continues – we go to
another part of the stage where
Elder Price is on a crappy hospital
bed.*

*An X-RAY comes up for all the
audience to see. It is of Price's
lower body, and we can clearly
see that the Book of Mormon has
been violently shoved up his ass.*

Then finally, the Doctor sings –

GOTSWANA
(singing softly)

SOMETHING INCREDIBLE...
YOU DID SOMETHING
    INCREDIBLE...
I HAVE NEVER SEEN A RECTAL
    BLOCKAGE OF THIS KIND.
I'VE SEEN PATIENTS IN THE PAST,
WITH RODENTS OR BOTTLES IN
    THEIR ASS,
BUT THIS IS SOMETHING
    INCREDIBLE,
AND IT BLOWS MY FUCKING MIND.

*Back to the "I Am Africa" song
with the Mormon boys.*

ELDERS

WE ARE THE SNOWS OF
    KILIMANJARO
WE ARE GORILLAS IN THE MIST
WE ARE THE GALLEYS OF THE
    AMISTAD
WE ARE FELA'S DEFIANT FIST!
WE ARE AFRICA!

*Now Cunningham and Nabulungi
step forward into their own light.*

ELDER CUNNINGHAM
It's just AMAZING, Neosporin! The
mission president wants to meet ME
personally! He's going to give me a
MEDAL!

NABULUNGI
Oh, Elder! That is INCREDIBLE!

*Cunningham and Nabulungi run
off.*

ELDERS

WE ARE AFRICA,
THE ZEBRA AND GIRAFFE-RICA.

*Now a part of the stage where The
General stands with one guard.*

THE GENERAL
Are you telling me EVERYONE
in the village is now joining some
religious CULT?! They must be
trying to power up their clitorises
to oppose me. I WILL KILL THEM
ALL!!!

ELDERS

WE ARE AFRICA
WE ARE AFRICA, WE ARE THE ONE,
    THE ONLY AFRICA
THE ONE AND ONLY AFRICA
AND THE LIFE WE LIVE
    IS PRIMITIVE AND PROUD

WITH MY ZUL
BAREFOOT THR
I A
AFR

ELDER MCKINLEY, ELDER CHURCH & ELDER ZELDER

LET US SMILE AND LAUGH-RICA

ELDERS

WE ARE AFRICA

WE ARE DEEPEST DARKEST AFRICA

SO DEEP AND DARK IN AFRICA

WE ARE FIELDS AND FERTILE

FORESTS WELL-ENDOWED!

WE ARE AFRICA.

ELDER MCKINLEY

WE ARE THE SUNRISE ON THE

SAVANNAH

ELDER ZELDER

A MONKEY WITH A BANANA

ELDER CHURCH

A TRIBAL WOMAN WHO DOESN'T

WEAR A BRA

ELDERS

AHHH AFRICANS ARE AFRICAN,

BUT WE ARE AFRICA!

- A KAFE IN KITGULI -

Price is sitting on a stool at the bar of some shitty counter. There are coffee cups lined up in front of him. Price is just finishing the last sip of coffee like it's scotch – his leg is trembling.

ELDER PRICE

Hit me up... Another one. COME ON!

The bartender finally pours him another cup and Price slams it.

Cunngingham walks up just in time to see Price start chugging

his twelfth cup of coffee.

ELDER CUNNINGHAM

Elder Price? You alright?

ELDER PRICE

Well, well... If it isn't the SUPER MORMON. Spreading "the word"?! Making more – BRAINWASHED zombies?!

ELDER CUNNINGHAM

Elder Price, what's happened to you?

ELDER PRICE

I WOKE UP, that's what happened!

ELDER CUNNINGHAM

Of course you woke up, you drank TWELVE CUPS OF COFFEE.

ELDER PRICE

(gets up)

How is it, huh?! You tell me how it is that YOU converted ALL those people into Mormons!

ELDER CUNNINGHAM

I don't know. Once I baptized Nagasaki the others just fell into place.

Price looks extra hurt.

ELDER PRICE

YOU get everything you pray for. YOU do all the things I was supposed to do. Doesn't that seem a LITTLE telling to you?!

ELDER CUNNINGHAM

Telling of what?!

ELDER PRICE

That the universe doesn't work the way we were told!

Price steps downstage to have his monologue.

ELDER PRICE
When I was nine years old... My family took a trip to Orlando, Florida. It was the most wonderful, most magical place I had ever seen. I said to myself, "THIS is where I want to spend eternity!" My parents told me that if I made God proud, and did what the church told me, in Latter Days I could have whatever I wanted. So I WORKED and I WORKED. And even when I studied Mormon stories and thought, "That doesn't make ANY SENSE," I KEPT WORKING because I was told ONE DAY – I would get my reward!! PLANET ORLANDO. But what do I have now? I can't even get a ticket home...

ELDER CUNNINGHAM
Alright, uh, look... The mission president is coming, and if I'm without my companion, well, you know that looks very bad. So if you could just –

ELDER PRICE
Oh THAT'S why you came!

ELDER CUNNINGHAM
No! I CAME because I care and –

ELDER PRICE
(loudest thing yet)
BULL POOP!

This is like a slap in the face to both boys.

ELDER PRICE
(brings it down)
That's bull poop, Elder. And you know it.

ELDER CUNNINGHAM
I know we aren't the best companions, but if we can PLEASE just ACT like we're still together in front of the mission president, you can get your ticket home, I can get my medal and we never have to see each other again.

ELDER PRICE
FINE. But don't TALK to me and DON'T touch me.

ELDER CUNNINGHAM
FINE.

ELDER PRICE
FINE.

Cunningham walks away. Price takes a moment and stares off to the sky and sings.

ORLANDO

ELDER PRICE
ORLANDO...
ORLANDO...
I LOVED YOU ORLANDO.
YOUR BRIGHT LIGHTS
YOUR BIG DREAMS
YOUR PROMISES YOU COULDN'T
    KEEP.
ORLANDO, ORLANDO,
WITHOUT YOU, ORLANDO
I'M JUST A GUY
WHO WILL DIE
AND NEVER GO BACK TO
    YOU.

- OUTSIDE THE MORMON MISSIONARIES' LIVING QUARTERS -

A FORMAL VERSION OF "I AM AFRICA" PLAYS as the Elders are all lined up to receive their awards. The mission president parades in with his assistants.

MISSION PRESIDENT
Boys, you have all done the most amazing work on your missions! You are the GLEAMING EXAMPLES of Latter-Day Saints!

MORMON MEN
Praise Christ!

ELDERS
Alright! / We did it! / Thank you! / Etc.

MISSION PRESIDENT
And YOU two – Elder Price and Elder Cunningham. You are the most successful missionaries in all of Africa!

ELDER CUNNINGHAM
Thank you, sir
(sarcastic)
my companion was so VERY HELPFUL and THERE for me!

MORMON MEN
Praise Christ!

Nabulungi bursts into the center of the room with the villagers.

NABULUNGI
Excuse me! Excuse me – Mr. Mormon President! My people wish to give you a special welcome!

ELDER CUNNINGHAM
Nabulungi, what are you doing?

NABULUNGI
We have learned so much from Elder Cunningham, and as our gift to you, we wish to present the story of Joseph Smit and the first Mormons!

The Mormon leaders CLAP.

ELDER CUNNINGHAM
UH NO!!! NO! I THINK THAT'S A BAD IDEA! Let's NOT DO THIS!

ELDER MCKINLEY
No, no, no, Elder! This is JUST THE KIND OF THING the Mormon leaders NEED to be seeing!

MISSION PRESIDENT
Yes, let's see what these noble Africans have learned!

ELDERS
Alright! / Cool! / Awesome! / Etc.

JOSEPH SMITH AMERICAN MOSES

NABULUNGI
AND NOW, we wish to honor you

with – the story of JOSEPH SMIT –
THE AMERICAN MOSES!!!!

MISSION PRESIDENT
OH! THIS IS VERY GOOD!!!

UGANDANS
MORMON!

NABULUNGI
I'm going to take you back in time.

UGANDANS
MORMON!

NABULUNGI
To the United States, 1823.

UGANDANS
MORMON!

NABULUNGI
A small and poor village called
Oopstate New York!

UGANDANS
OOPSTATE.

NABULUNGI
There was disease and famine.

UGANDANS
SO SICK.

NABULUNGI
But also in this village lived a simple
farmer who would change everything.
His name...was Joseph Smit.

UGANDANS
YA YA YA YA YA YA YA YA YA YA YA!
JOSEPH SMIT
AMERICAN MOSES.
PRAISE BE TO JOSEPH,
AMERICAN PROPHET MAN.

JOSEPH SMITH (MUTUMBO)
Ay, my name is Joseph Smit. I'm
going to fuck this baby.

MISSION PRESIDENT
WHAT?!?!

UGANDANS
NO, NO, JOSEPH!
DON'T FUCK DA BABY!
JOSEPH SMIT
DON'T FUCK DA BABY!

NABULUNGI
Suddenly the clouds parted! And
Joseph Smit was visited by GOD!

{ 83 }

GOD (MAFALA)
JOSEPH SMIT!
DO NOT FUCK A BABY.
I'LL GET RID OF YOUR AIDS
IF YOU FUCK DIS FROG.

UGANDANS
YA YA YA YA YA YA YA YA YA YA YA!

NABULUNGI
Joseph Smit fucked the frog God gave to him and his AIDS went away! And then, a great wizard named Moroni appeared from the Starship Enterprise!

MORONI (MIDDALA)
Joseph Smit. Your village is shit. You shall lead your villagers to a new village. TAKE THESE FUCKING GOLDEN PLATES!

UGANDANS
OH-WAY!

NABULUNGI
And on the plates were written the directions to a new land – SALT-TALAAAAY- KA SITI!

UGANDANS
SAL-TALAAAAA KA SITI!

NABULUNGI
Joseph tried to convince ALL the villagers to follow him and his golden plates!

JOSEPH SMITH
Liberation! Equality! No more slavery for Oopstate Mormon people!
I GOT THE GOLDEN PLATES.

UGANDANS
GOLD PLATES

JOSEPH SMITH
GONNA LEAD THE PEOPLE

UGANDANS
WE HEAD WEST

JOSEPH SMITH
WE GOTTA STICK TOGEDDAH

UGANDANS
MORMONS!

JOSEPH SMITH
WE GOTTA HELP EACH UDDAH

UGANDANS
WE'RE MORMONS!

JOSEPH SMITH
AND SO WE CLIMB THE MOUNTAIN

UGANDANS
WE HEAD WEST!

JOSEPH SMITH
AND WE CROSS THE RIVER

UGANDANS
WE HEAD WEST!

JOSEPH SMITH
AND WE FIGHT THE OPPRESSION

UGANDANS

MORMONS!

JOSEPH SMITH

BY BEING NICE TO EV'RY ONE

UGANDANS

WE'RE MORMONS!

**BRIGHAM YOUNG
(GOTSWANA)**

Not so fast, Mormons! You shall not pass MY mountain!

UGANDANS

Down from the mountain, look who comes! The American warlord, Brigham Young!

BRIGHAM YOUNG

Yes, I am Brigham Young! I cut off my daughter's clitoris! That made God angry so he turned my nose into a clit for punishment!

UGANDANS

BRIGHAM YOUNG!

HIS NOSE WAS A CLITORIS.

WHAT WILL YOU DO, JOSEPH?

WILL YOU FIGHT THE CLITORIS

MAN?

JOSEPH SMITH

Not fight him...Help him.

UGANDANS

Ohhh!

NABULUNGI

Joseph Smit took his magical fuck frog and rubbed it upon Brigham Young's clit face. And behold, Brigham was CURED!

UGANDANS

JOSEPH SMIT - MAGICAL AIDS

FROG

BRIGHAM YOUNG - FROG ON HIS

CLIT FACE

NABULUNGI

Brigham Young was so grateful, he decided to JOIN the Mormons on their journey!

JOSEPH SMITH

Compassion!

BRIGHAM YOUNG

Courtesy!

JOSEPH SMITH

Let's be really fucking polite to everyone!

I GOT THE GOLDEN PLATES!

UGANDANS

GOLD PLATES

JOSEPH SMITH

GONNA LEAD THE PEOPLE

UGANDANS

WE HEAD WEST!

BRIGHAM YOUNG

WE GOTTA STICK TOGEDDAH

UGANDANS

MORMONS!

NABULUNGI

Now comes the part of our story that gets a little bit sad.

UGANDANS

Ohhhh...

NABULUNGI

After traveling for so long, the Mormons ran out of fresh water. And became sick...with DYSENTERY!

UGANDANS

MORMON GO TO DA WATAH,
WATAH GO TO DA CUP.
CUP GO TO DA STOMACH,
SHIT COME OUT DA BUTT.
SHIT GO IN DA WATAH,
WATAH GO IN DA CUP.
SHIT GO DOWN DA STOMACH,
SHIT COME OUT DA BUTT.

JOSEPH SMITH

Oh fuck!

NABULUNGI

Oh no! The prophet Joseph Smit is now getting sick!

UGANDANS

SHIT GO IN DA WATAH,
WATAH GO IN DA CUP.
CUP GO TO DA THIRSTY,
SHIT GO TO DA STOMACH,
BLOOD COME OUT DA BUTT.
BLOOD GO IN DA WATAH,
WATAH GO IN DA CUP.
CUP GO TO DA THROAT.
SHIT BLOOD IN DA STOMACH,
SHIT BLOOD IN DA MOUTH.
SHIT BLOOD ON DA INSIDES,
WATAH COME OUT DA BUTT!

JOSEPH SMITH

Augh! Brigham Young! You take the golden plates and lead the Mormons to the promised land!

BRIGHAM YOUNG

Desperation! Mortality! Loss of Faith! Ahhhh –

GOT DE GOLDEN PLATES

UGANDANS

GOLD PLATES

BRIGHAM YOUNG

GONNA LEAD DE PEOPLE

UGANDANS

WE HEAD WEST!

BRIGHAM YOUNG

WE GOTTA STICK TOGEDDAH

UGANDANS

MORMONS!

NABULUNGI

Even though their prophet had died,

the Mormons stuck together and helped each other...

BRIGHAM YOUNG

WE GOTTA HELP EACH UDDAH

UGANDANS

WE'RE MORMONS.
WE HEAD WEST.

NABULUNGI
...And were really nice to everyone they came across.

UGANDANS

WE HEAD WEST!
MORMONS!

NABULUNGI
And then one day, the Mormons finally FOUND Sal Tlay Ka Siti!

UGANDANS

SAL TLAY KA SITI!!!!

NABULUNGI
And there, the Mormons danced with Ewoks! And were greeted by Jesus!

JESUS (GHALI)
Welcome, Mormons! Now let's all have as MANY BABIES AS WE CAN! To make BIG MORMON FAMILIES!!!!

UGANDANS

FUCK YOUR WOMAN
FUCK YOUR MAN,
IT IS ALL PART OF GOD'S PLAN,
MORMONS FUCK ALL THAT THEY
CAN
HERE IN SAL TLAY KA SITI LAND!
THANK YOU, THANK YOU GOD!
(NOW WE ARE FUCKING)
THANK YOU, THANK YOU GOD!
(GOD WANTS US FUCKING)

THANK YOU, THANK YOU GOD!
(GET BACK TO FUCKING)
THANK YOU, THANK YOU GOD!
JOSEPH SMIT FUCK FROG,
BRIGHAM YOUNG CLIT FACE,
SHIT COME OUT DE BUTT,
JESUS SAYS FUCK FUCK
MORMONS!!!!!!

The song ends and all the white people just look horrified and in shock.

MISSION PRESIDENT
ELDERS... I'd like to have a word with you all... NOW!!!!

The mission president and the committee storm out of the room. The Elders all follow. Then finally, after they are gone:

MUTUMBO
I THINK THEY LIKED IT!!!

UGANDANS
Yeah! / Alright! / We did it! / Etc.

The furious mission president and LDS leaders are alone with the Elders.

ELDER MCKINLEY
We are sorry, mission president! We had no idea –

MISSION PRESIDENT
YOU KEEP YOUR MOUTH SHUT! YOU'RE IN ENOUGH TROUBLE AS IT IS!

ELDER CUNNINGHAM
Sir, I was just trying to help the villagers! They all really wanted to learn.

Nabulungi walks in with a large manuscript.

NABULUNGI
Elder?! Elder, I wanted to give you this! It's the entire play written in text!

She looks at all the long faces.

NABULUNGI
What's going on?

Silence.

MISSION PRESIDENT
What's going on is that you have all brought ridicule down onto the Latter-Day Saints!

NABULUNGI
But...we are ALL Latter-Day Saints now, right?

MISSION PRESIDENT
YOU AND YOUR PEOPLE ARE ABOUT AS FAR FROM BEING LATTER-DAY SAINTS AS IT GETS!
(turns to the missionaries)
YOU ALL ARE!

NABULUNGI
Elder Cunningham, TELL THEM! We are ready to go to Sal Tlay Ka Siti! My things are packed!

ELDER CUNNINGHAM
Nabulungi, I'm so sorry – I never meant that you were ACTUALLY going to Salt Lake –

NABULUNGI
-But you said WE could find paradise by listening to you!

ELDER CUNNINGHAM
When we say that we mean paradise within YOURSELF – you know it's like a – a Jesus thing.

NABULUNGI
(extremely hurt)
Oh... I see... So when you baptized me...it meant nothing?

ELDER CUNNINGHAM
It meant EVERYTHING!

NABULUNGI
Everyone disobeyed The General because I told them to listen to you! Where are uncircumcised women supposed to go now?!

Cunningham stammers as he looks to the Elders for help.

ELDER CUNNINGHAM
Wul, no...We're gonna stay here and help *(to other Elders)* Right?

NABULUNGI
I KNOW what you people are now. You travel from your sparkling, lovely paradise in Ootah to tell ridiculous stories to people less fortunate. To make fun of them.

ELDER CUNNINGHAM
It isn't like that!

NABULUNGI
You have crushed my soul.
...I hope you all had a good laugh.

MISSION PRESIDENT
ELDERS! You may as well PACK YOUR THINGS. This district is SHUT DOWN. You'll be given tickets home and you can EXPLAIN to your parents you have ALL FAILED as missionaries!

Sad and pounding Les

*Misérables "Look Down" music
starts to play.*

Nabulungi runs out.

HASA DIGA EEBOWAI
(SAD REPRISE)

*Nabulungi is left alone on
the stage holding her Book of
Mormon...silence and stillness...*

NABULUNGI

I WAS SUCH A FOOL TO HAVE
    FOLLOWED THIS ADVICE.
THERE IS NO TRIP TO PARADISE.
HOW COULD I LET MY HOPE GET
    SO HIGH...?

*She looks up to the sky and pauses
just a beat before singing –*

NABULUNGI

HASA DIGA ... EEBOWAI.

Now she belts it out.

NABULUNGI

HASA DIGA EEBOWAI!
YOU GAVE ME A DREAM BUT IT WAS
    ALL A LIE.
I THINK YOU LIKE TO SEE ME CRY.
    HASA DIGA...

*She can't finish, so she runs off,
crying.*

Cunningham and Price enter.

ELDER CUNNINGHAM
(about to cry)
Boy... I really did it this time, huh? I

mean... I've always been a screw up
but THIS –

ELDER PRICE
Joseph Smith dying of dysentery?
Moroni from the Starship
Enterprise? That play...was the most
MIRACULOUS thing I've ever seen!

ELDER CUNNINGHAM
Huh?

Price crosses to Cunningham.

ELDER PRICE
I mean, it was a bunch of made-up
stuff but it POINTED to something
bigger, and–

*MUSIC STING. Elder Price
suddenly seems to get it –*

ELDER PRICE
Wait a minute... You little SNEAK!
You've been trying to teach me
something all along, haven't you?!

ELDER CUNNINGHAM
(confused)
What?

ELDER PRICE
I thought I could fly in here and
change everything. But I made it all
about ME. While I was losing faith,
you went and did–

SOMETHING INCREDIBLE

ELDER PRICE

SOMETHING INCREDIBLE.
YOU DID SOMETHING

INCREDIBLE...
FOR A PEOPLE WHO HAD
    NOWHERE ELSE TO GO ...
I THOUGHT THEY WERE
    UNREACHABLE –
BUT THEN THEY WERE HAPPY AND
    HOPEFUL AND WEARING
    COSTUMES
IT WAS ALMOST LIKE...
    ORLANDO...

Sorry it took me so long to realize what you were trying to teach me, Elder.

ELDER CUNNINGHAM
(not really understanding)
Oh, that's okay.

Cunningham gives another look to show that he has no idea what Price is talking about.

ELDER CUNNINGHAM
But what about that poor girl?! I– I made her believe in a bunch of made-up crap!

ELDER PRICE
It doesn't matter if the stories are true or not. That isn't the point...

ELDER CUNNINGHAM
No, it doesn't MATTER now cuz she's gonna get her clit cut off and it's all my fault!

ELDER PRICE
No, come on, Elder! You can't give up now! We have to try and FIX THIS!

Price leads Cunningham offstage.

- THE VILLAGE -

Back in the Ugandan village, the people all wait as Nabulungi enters.

MAFALA
So what did the Mormon president think of our play?

MUTUMBO
Did Elder Cunningham like it?

The General enters, with one of his guards.

THE GENERAL
JUMAMOSI!

The Ugandans huddle together in fear.

UGANDANS
(random screaming and fear)

THE GENERAL
There have been RUMORS that the people in this village are uniting to oppose me.

MUTUMBO
Yes, we have been shown another way!

But Nabulungi steps in front of him.

NABULUNGI
No... NO! We do not oppose you... We will do what you say.

MUTUMBO
Nabulungi, what's wrong? Our prophet has taught us to stick together and FIGHT oppression!

NABULUNGI
Forget about Elder Cunningham. You aren't going to see him ever again.

MIDDALA
What?! Why not?

NABULUNGI
Because Elder Cunningham...he was eaten by lions, alright?

UGANDANS
Lions? What?

GOTSWANA
Our prophet was eaten by lions???

THE GENERAL
ENOUGH! There is ONE LAW you will obey here, and it is MINE!

MIDDALA
We believe in something ELSE!

NABULUNGI
STOP IT, ALL OF YOU! I told you, our prophet is gone! There is no promised land. There is no salvation.

SADAKA
NO! You must not talk like that Nabulungi. Remember the teachings of the first Mormons. When Joseph Smit died they did not give up on their hope.

NABULUNGI
But it's not TRUE. We aren't going to Sal Tlay Ka Siti.

KIMBAY
Nabulungi, Sal Tlay Ka Siti isn't an actual PLACE... It's an IDEA. A metaphor.

MAFALA
You need to remember that prophets ALWAYS speak in metaphors.

UGANDAN WOMAN
Yeah, you don't think a man ACTUALLY fucked a frog, do you? That's fucking stupid.

NABULUNGI
And you all believe this?

UGANDANS
Yes!

Elder Price and Cunningham enter the village.

ELDER CUNNINGHAM
Excuse me, everyone –

UGANDANS
(GASP)

MIDDALA
He is risen!

KALIMBA
It is a miracle!

MAFALA
Our prophet returns even from the dead!
(to The General)
THERE, YOU SEE?!

UGANDAN WOMAN
He must have fucked a frog!

THE GENERAL
Who has risen from the dead?!

ELDER PRICE
HE HAS, you IDIOT! So you might as well PUT THAT GUN DOWN BECAUSE IT WILL NOT WORK AGAINST THE UNDEAD. And if you do not get OUT of this village he WILL command the angel Moroni, ON the Death Star, to unleash the Kraken! Which will then... Uh...

ELDER CUNNINGHAM
Which will then – fire Joseph Smith torpedoes FROM its mouth of Christ and turn YOU into a LESBIAN!

ELDER PRICE
Oh – don't think he can't do it.

The General runs off.

UGANDANS
Alright! / Yeah! / We did it! / Etc.

ELDER CUNNINGHAM
Oh Nala, I am so sorry. But please, if you just give me a chance –

Nabulungi puts her hand over Cunningham's mouth.

NABULUNGI
Elder, it's okay... I understand now what you have been trying to teach me all along.

ELDER CUNNINGHAM
(still confused)
Oh, okay. Great.

Cunningham and Nabulungi hug.

The other Elders all walk in, rolling carry-on bags.

ELDER PRICE
Woa – woa Elders where are you going?

ELDER MCKINLEY
What do you mean "Where are we going?" We've been shut down!

ELDER NEELEY
Yeah, we have to go home!

ELDER PRICE
Who says we have to?

ELDER ZELDER
What?

Price gets in the middle of everyone.

ELDER PRICE
Look, we all wanted to go on a mission so we could spend two years of our lives helping people out. So let's DO it!

ELDER NEELEY
But the mission president said we're all as far from Latter-Day Saints as it gets!

ELDER PRICE
No... You know what guys? FUCK HIM.

Everyone looks a little shocked.

ELDER PRICE
We are STILL Latter-Day Saints. ALL of us. Even if we change some things, or break the rules, or have complete doubt that God exists... We can still work together to make THIS our paradise planet.

ELDER CUNNINGHAM
You wanna stay here with me?

ELDER PRICE
I'd do anything for you. I'm your best friend.

Cunningham smiles and dives into Price with a big hug. A chime, and then Price steps forward to sing:

ELDER PRICE
    DON'T WORRY LITTLE BUDDY.
    KNOW THIS MUCH IS TRUE.
    TOMORROW IS A LATTER DAY

**ELDER PRICE &
ELDER CUNNINGHAM**
    AND I AM HERE FOR YOU.

TOMORROW IS A LATTER DAY

ELDER MCKINLEY
    TOMORROW IS A LATTER DAY...

ELDERS
    TOMORROW IS A LATTER DAY!
    TOMORROW IS A LATTER DAY!

(Intro dance break)

ELDER PRICE
    I AM A LATTER-DAY SAINT!
    I HELP ALL THOSE I CAN!

ELDER CUNNINGHAM
    AND SEE MY FRIENDS THROUGH
        TIMES OF JOY AND SORROW.

ELDER PRICE
    WHO CARES WHAT HAPPENS
        WHEN WE'RE DEAD?
    WE SHOULDN'T THINK THAT FAR
        AHEAD.

**ELDER PRICE &
ELDER CUNNINGHAM**
    THE ONLY LATTER DAY THAT
        MATTERS IS TOMORROW!

ELDERS
    THE SKIES ARE CLEARING AND
        THE SUN'S COMING OUT.
    IT'S A LATTER DAY TOMORROW!

UGANDANS
    HAYYA YA!

ELDERS
    PUT YOUR WORRIES AND YOUR
        SORROWS
    AND YOUR CARES AWAY
    AND FOCUS ON THE LATTER DAY!

TOMOR

LAT

DA

OW IS A

TER

Y!

ENTIRE COMPANY
TOMORROW IS A LATTER DAY!
WOO!

NABULUNGI
I AM A LATTER-DAY SAINT
ALONG WITH ALL MY TOWN.
WE ALWAYS STICK TOGETHER
COME WHAT MAY!

ENTIRE COMPANY
SHOODOOWOW!
BA DA BA!
BA DA BA!
WANNA THANK YOU LORD!

ELDER MCKINLEY
WE LOVE TO DANCE AND SHOUT
AND LET ALL OUR FEELINGS OUT!

MORMONS
AND WORK TO MAKE A BETTER
LATTER

ENTIRE COMPANY
DAY!

UGANDANS
HANNA HEYA HA HANNA HEYA

ENTIRE COMPANY
WE'RE GONNA BE HERE FOR EACH
OTHER EVERY STEP OF THE WAY
AND MAKE A LATTER DAY
TOMORROW!

UGANDANS
HANNA HEY!
AMERICANS ALREADY FOUND A
CURE FOR AIDS
BUT THEY'RE SAVING IT FOR A
LATTER DAY!

ENTIRE COMPANY
YEAH!
TOMORROW IS A LATTER DAY!

ELDER PRICE
I BELIEVE!
I BELIEVE!
I BELIEVE!

ENTIRE COMPANY
TOMORROW IS A LATTER DAY!
LOVE AND JOY AND ALL THE
THINGS THAT MATTER DAY!
TOMORROW IS A BIGGER BADDER
LATTER DAY!

**ELDER PRICE &
ELDER CUNNINGHAM**
I BELIEVE
I BELIEVE
I BELIEVE

ENTIRE COMPANY
TOMORROW, TOMORROW IS A
LATTER DAY,
A HAPPY ENDING ON A PLATTER
DAY
TOMORROW'S A DOPER, PHATTER
LATTER DAY
WHY ARE MORMONS HAPPY?
IT'S BECAUSE WE KNOW

IT'S A LATTER DAY TOMORROW.
SO IF YOU'RE SAD,
PUT YOUR HANDS TOGETHER AND
    PRAY
    THAT TOMORROW'S GONNA BE A
    LATTER DAY!
IT PROBABLY WILL BE A LATTER
    DAY!
TOMORROW IS A LATTER DAY!

ELDER CUNNINGHAM

SO WHAT WILL TOMORROW BRING?

ELDER PRICE

WHAT DOES THE FUTURE HOLD?

NABULUNGI / PRICE / CUNNINGHAM

I CAN ALMOST SEE IT NOW...

One of the Ugandans suddenly appears wearing a white shirt and black tie as the song transforms –

HELLO
(REPRISE)

MUTUMBO

HELLO! MY NAME IS ELDER
    MUTUMBO!
AND I WOULD LIKE TO SHARE
    WITH YOU
    THE MOST AMAZING BOOK!

KIMBAY

HELLO!

GOTSWANA

HELLO!

KIMBAY

MY NAME IS SISTER KIMBAY!
IT'S A BOOK ABOUT A PEOPLE WHO
    WERE POOR AND SAD LIKE YOU!

NABULUNGI

A SACRED TEXT –

MAFALA

HELLO!

NABULUNGI

– OF PIONEERS AND FROGS

MAFALA

FUCKED FROGS!

NABULUNGI

AND HOW YOU CAN FIND
    SALVATION IF YOU JUST BELIEVE.

UGANDAN WOMAN

HI HO!

KIMBAY AND MIDDALA

DING DONG!

KALIMBA

HELLO!

UGANDAN WOMAN

BOBA FETT!

KALIMBA

YOU HAVE A LOVELY MUD HUT.
AND IF YOU JUST PUT DOWN THE
    GUN I'LL SHOW YOU -
OH OKAY I'LL LEAVE.

SADAKA

HELLO!

GHALI

HELLO! MY NAME IS ELDER GHALI.
YOU WILL LOVE ALL OF THE

**HAPPINESS THIS BOOK CAN
BRING.**

THE GENERAL
HELLO.

MIDDALA
HELLO!

THE GENERAL
MY NAME IS ELDER BUTT-FUCKING
NAKED.
DID YOU KNOW THAT THE
CLITORIS IS A HOLY SACRED
THING?

UGANDANS
FIND PARADISE!

KIMBAY
WITH JESUS CHRIST!

UGANDANS
AND NO MORE WAR!

THE GENERAL
HELLO!

MIDDALA
NICE DOOR!

UGANDANS
YOU'VE READ THE BOOK OF
MORMON
DID YOU KNOW THERE'S MORE?

NABULUNGI
PART FOUR!

UGANDANS
WE SWEAR –

THE GENERAL
WE REALLY CARE.

UGANDANS
THIS IS NOT A SCAM.

THE GENERAL
NO, MA'AM.

UGANDANS
HAVE YOU HEARD THE STORY
OF OUR PROPHET ARNOLD
CUNNINGHAM?
ARNOLD CUNNINGHAM?
HELLO!
ARNOLD CUNNING...

ELDER CUNNINGHAM
*(entering, followed by all the
Mormons)*
HELL-O!!!!!

ENTIRE COMPANY
HELLO! OUR CHURCH IS GROWING
STRONG!
AND IF YOU LET US IN WE'LL SHOW YOU
HOW YOU CAN BELONG!
JOIN OUR FAMILY.
AND SET YOUR SPIRIT FREE.
WE CAN FULLY GUARANTEE YOU
THAT
THIS BOOK WILL CHANGE YOUR LIFE.
THIS BOOK WILL CHANGE YOUR LIFE.
THIS BOOK WILL CHANGE YOUR LIFE.
THIS BOOK WILL CHANGE YOUR LIFE.
THE BOOK OF ARNOLD.
HELLO!

*The entire company joyously
raises high the BOOK OF
ARNOLD.*